## *His glass had been refilled for the third time when he saw her.*

She looked left, then right. When their eyes locked, Lucky watched her slip through the crowd, her shiny black hair moving around her slender shoulders.

She wasn't dressed to be noticed, but that didn't stop the men from taking a second look. She had an angel's face, with a walk that would make a man follow her to hell and back on his knees. He'd been around plenty of beautiful women over the years, but this woman had everything. Too much of everything, he decided, as his gaze focused on her V-neck sweater and the way it was doing a damn fine job of framing her assets.

It occurred to him as he glanced around the room that every guy in the place was anticipating Elena strutting down the catwalk, that she was assumed to be a dancer looking for a job.

Only they both knew she wasn't there to work the crowd. She was there to work *him*.

Dear Reader,

Welcome to another month of the most exciting romantic reading around, courtesy of Silhouette Intimate Moments. Starting things off with a bang, we have *To Love a Thief* by ultrapopular Merline Lovelace. This newest CODE NAME: DANGER title takes you back into the supersecret world of the Omega Agency for a dangerous liaison you won't soon forget.

For military romance, Catherine Mann's WINGMEN WARRIORS are the ones to turn to. These uniformed heroes and heroines are irresistible, and once you join Darcy Renshaw and Max Keagan for a few *Private Maneuvers,* you won't even be trying to resist, anyway. Wendy Rosnau continues her unflashed miniseries THE BROTHERHOOD in *Last Man Standing,* while Sharon Mignerey's couple find themselves *In Too Deep.* Finally, welcome two authors who are new to the line but not to readers. Kristen Robinette makes an unforgettable entrance with *In the Arms of a Stranger,* and Ana Leigh offers a matchup between *The Law and Lady Justice.*

I hope you enjoy all six of these terrific novels, and that you'll come back next month for more of the most electrifying romantic reading around.

Enjoy!

Leslie J. Wainger
Executive Editor

Please address questions and book requests to:
Silhouette Reader Service
U.S.: 3010 Walden Ave., P.O. Box 1325, Buffalo, NY 14269
Canadian: P.O. Box 609, Fort Erie, Ont. L2A 5X3

# Last Man Standing

## WENDY ROSNAU

Silhouette®

INTIMATE MOMENTS™

Published by Silhouette Books

America's Publisher of Contemporary Romance

**SILHOUETTE BOOKS**

ISBN 0-373-27297-9

LAST MAN STANDING

Copyright © 2003 by Wendy Rosnau

This edition published by arrangement with Harlequin Books S.A.

® and TM are trademarks of Harlequin Books S.A., used under license.
Trademarks indicated with ® are registered in the United States Patent
and Trademark Office, the Canadian Trade Marks Office and in other
countries.

Visit us at www.eHarlequin.com

**Printed in U.S.A.**

## WENDY ROSNAU

resides on sixty secluded acres in Minnesota with her husband and their two children. She divides her time between her family-owned bookstore and writing romantic suspense.

Her first book, *The Long Hot Summer,* was a *Romantic Times* nominee for Best First Series Romance of 2000. Her third book, *The Right Side of the Law*, was a *Romantic Times* Top Pick. She received the Midwest Fiction Writers 2001 Rising Star Award.

Wendy loves to hear from her readers. Visit her Web site at www.wendyrosnau.com.

To my husband, Jerry,
who continues to stand beside me.
I love you....

# Chapter 1

Each time Lucky Masado entered the gates of Dante Armanno, he found one more reason not to like Vito Tandi's estate. Today's niggle was security.

There were nine state-of-the-art cameras positioned strategically on the grounds, two twelve-foot electronic iron gates, eight hungry-looking Rottweilers on the prowl and four experienced *soldatos* shouldering AR-70s on the rooftop.

Still, he'd been inside the house twice without anyone knowing, which meant any day of the week he could play gut-and-run on Vito Tandi and walk away. But that's not what Lucky wanted from the old capo. Vito would die soon enough without anyone cutting his jugular. If he lasted the year, it would be a miracle.

The armed guard at the gate was expecting Lucky and flagged him through. It was late, after nine, and he drove his red Ferrari—the only extravagant toy he owned—up the paved half-mile driveway lined with one-hundred-year-old oak trees dressed in winter white.

Yesterday, two days after Thanksgiving, the Midwest had gotten ten inches of snow. With temperatures tickling twenty degrees, it was logical to assume that winter had arrived in Chicago.

Lucky sped through the second set of open gates—another guard giving him a nod—then rounded the circular inlaid courtyard where the statue of Armanno, Sicily's legendary hero, stood in a snowdrift.

Accustomed to the routine that had been set a few days ago, he climbed out of the car, tossed his keys to a man named Finch and headed for the keystone archway. He was still required to empty his pockets at the front door. Lucky pulled out his weapons. Three knives—a Hibben, four-inch stiletto and a Haug with a curved blade able to tear a man to shreds in a matter of seconds—were laid out on a marble slab inside the archway. Next came the guns: two skeleton-grip 9-mm Berettas, a Smith & Wesson .22 and the *lupara* that rode inside the lining of his jacket.

His pockets empty, Lucky entered the house and followed Vito's bodyguard down a hallway lit by shadow boxes filled with everything from sixteenth-century swords to Civil War rifles. Vito's bodyguard was a foot taller than Lucky, which put him over seven feet. Dressed in black pants and a black sweater, the only hint that Benito Palone lived for more than protecting the life of a dying mob boss was the diamond earring he wore and the tattoo of a woman's backside burned into his forearm.

Lucky had noticed the earring days ago. Now as Benito reached to open the study door, he offered Lucky a glimpse of his tattoo, two inches above his wrist.

Because Lucky knew Palone's intent was to follow him inside, he turned before the big man had a chance to duck his head and negotiate the door's six-nine opening. Then, in a voice much quieter than one would expect for a man reported to be the most aggressive street soldier in Chicago, he said, "Not this time, Palone. Today, I'm a solo act with your boss."

The guard's green eyes narrowed. He looked over Lucky's head to where the ailing mobster sat behind an eight-foot-long oak desk. "What do you say, Mr. Tandi? He has no weapons, but—"

"It's all right, Benito," Vito's gravelly voice rumbled. "If Frank Masado's son was going to kill me, I expect I would be dead by now. Isn't that right, Nine-Lives Lucky?"

Lucky refused to be baited by the use of his childhood nickname. Since he had established himself in the organization years ago, his nickname had been shortened. Of course there were those who still used his given name of Tomas—mostly people outside the *famiglia.*

"You wanted to see me." Lucky eyed the bulky body behind the desk. Vito was dressed in a black smoking jacket with red satin lapels. He was sixty-three years old and bald, but for a graying tuft that rimmed the back of his head and tickled his ears. He was average in height, well above average in weight and would be dead within the year of throat cancer.

"My lawyer made the changes you requested in my will. The papers were delivered this afternoon. They're ready to be signed."

Two days ago Lucky had agreed to become Vito Tandi's son on paper—the heir of Dante Armanno. That is, if certain sections of the will were amended to his specifications.

CEO of Vito's fortune had never made Lucky's list of dream jobs. But being born Sicilian and the son of a syndicate player hadn't been something he could control. Liking who and what you were wasn't a requirement for doing the job you were trained to do, his father had always told him. Not when he was twenty, and not now at thirty-one.

Vito raised his hand and motioned for Lucky to take a seat in the red velvet chair in front of his desk. Then, with a gratuitous wave, he shooed away his guard. "Benito, tell Summ to bring us something to drink. I believe there will be cause to celebrate. Tell her we'd like—"

"Scotch," Lucky suggested, shedding his brown leather jacket. He dropped it beside the chair before taking a seat.

"It looks like we need to restock the wine cellar, Benito. I've neglected it this past year, and I imagine it's in sorry shape." Vito studied Lucky for a moment and finally said, "Your preferences?"

"Macallan, and some good wine."

"Yes, I'm a wine man myself. Bardolino and soave." His gaze went back to his bodyguard. "There you have it, Benito. Make arrangements to restock the cellar. And instruct Summ to bring us the best Scotch we have in the house."

When the door closed, Vito reached for a fat Italian cigar in a carved wooden box. "Cigar?"

Lucky shook his head. "Just the Scotch."

"The other day when I suggested you move into the estate as soon as possible, I sensed some reluctance. I understand you still live in your father's old house. After tonight, I suspect, your enemies will double. This would be the safest place for you, huh?"

Lucky said nothing. He wasn't going to sell the house

in town. He and Joey had already discussed what they would do with it, if and when he moved out.

"It's no secret that money and power is not what drives you," Vito continued. "If it was, you would have moved out of your old neighborhood long ago. So what will it take to convince you to accept my generosity and live with me at Dante Armanno?"

Never short on words when he had something to say, Lucky said, "An overhaul on security, for starters, and a private meeting with each of your guards."

Vito's bushy eyebrows climbed his forehead. "My security expenditures are close to a million a year. Are you suggesting that's not enough?"

"There are things money can't buy. I'm sure you're aware of that."

His candid reference to Vito's failing health and his irreversible fate was duly noted with a sour grunt of displeasure.

"Your house has thirty-eight rooms, nine entrances and 116 windows," Lucky continued. "Twenty-one of those windows are in need of repairs. You also have a state-of-the-art underground tunnel. By the way, the light is out in the hidden passageway leading to your bedroom. Unless someone has replaced it since this morning."

"You've been busy. Am I to assume no tour will be necessary once you move in?"

"You can assume whatever you want, old man."

An unexpected rusty chuckle erupted from Vito. Rubbing his swollen hands together, he said, "This is better than I expected. Yes, very good." He waved his hand again. "Make any changes you feel necessary. Fire and hire. Do whatever it takes to make my home your home."

Lucky adjusted himself in the chair, wishing the housekeeper would hurry up with the Scotch. His back hurt like a son of a bitch, and lately it was taking a lot more sauce to dull the pain.

"It's no secret that Carlo Talupa named Moody Trafano as my heir."

Lucky nodded. "My men tell me he's been smiling for weeks. He's also become a regular at the Shedd in anticipation of his takeover."

"Such a shame for Carlo to die so tragically." Vito's words didn't match his casual shrug. "His unfortunate death puts Moody Trafano out in the cold and now allows me to name my own heir."

There was still an ongoing investigation into the recent murder of Carlo Talupa. He'd been whacked and left in the back seat of a junked car at a salvage garage. He'd been missing for four days before he'd been found.

The police had no suspects, but Lucky didn't need to sift through Carlo's enemy list to know who had fired six bullets into the Chicago mob boss's head.

"You know Moody Trafano is a man without honor. A greedy moron." Vito's lips curled. "Weeks ago I explained this to Carlo, but he wasn't interested in my measure of his choice. I can only guess that he was honoring some deal he made with Vinnie."

Moody Trafano was Vincent D'Lano's bastard son. They were both slippery snakes looking for easy money and a paved road to the top of the syndicate ladder.

"If Carlo was alive, we would not be having this discussion," Vito conceded. "Moody would be still celebrating his elevated position."

"Then we can thank fate," Lucky said blandly, "for Carlo's timely death."

Vito puffed on his cigar and the room turned blue with smoke. "Fate. It is a hard word to define, huh?"

Lucky shrugged off the question.

"My father was born in Palermo. When he settled in Detroit, he hoped life would be good, but it was hard for him. I remember going to bed night after night hungry, rubbing my belly. I vowed when I got older and could work, never to be hungry again. I worked two jobs at age fourteen. Sixteen-hour days on the docks bought me food and eventually a home of my own. Respect. Years later I came here and bought the steel mill. I never went hungry after that, and neither did the men I recruited from the waterfront. Hungry men. Good men down on their luck. The harder they worked, the more I fed them. The loyalty of hardworking men…it is a winning combination, huh?"

Lucky agreed, but again said nothing.

"I learned all of my men's names and the names of their wives and children. I sent groceries to their homes. Bought gifts for their children at Christmas. I no longer visit the mill, but I still know my men by name. I still send food and gifts to their families. I have heard that you also believe in rewarding loyalty this way. That your men follow you out of love, as well as fear. A true *mafioso* knows that respect and honor is his responsibility, not his choice.

"Some say you enjoy watching a man bleed, Lucky. And it is true you honor the old ways and do what many have no stomach to do. But you are about more than spilling blood. You are feared because you know what it means to be a *un' uomo d'onore*. A man of honor. Your loyalty to your brother and Jackson Ward at age fifteen will never be forgotten."

"I did not know the price I would pay that night, old

man. I assure you, I wasn't thinking about the old ways in that alley. I went only to—"

"Protect your brother and friend from being killed by the local *cricca*," Vito finished. "Yes, I know the story. Three against a gang of ten, wasn't it?" One thick finger pointed to a scar half-hidden on Lucky's neck by his collar-length black hair. "I am told that the scar on your back stretches four feet in length."

"An exaggeration," Lucky disputed, knowing for a fact that the scar fell short by only two inches.

"The story claims they held you down and cut you while your brother and friend were made to watch. Is it true that you shot three of the *cricca* after the fact, or is that an exaggeration, too?"

That part wasn't an exaggeration. Lucky, however, wasn't proud of the fact that he'd caused three mothers to grieve and wail at their sons' funerals. Still, he had done what he had to do to save his brother and best friend.

The *cricca* thought they had killed him. Lucky had believed it, too. In what he thought were his last seconds on earth, he'd made one last stand to give Joey and Jackson a chance to survive.

He leaned back and slid his hand into the waistband of his jeans; inside his shorts, past his scarred belly to palm the second .22 he carried—the one responsible for saving all their lives that night in the alley. The gun that now permanently rode snug against him as comfortably as his wallet did in his back pocket.

Lucky pulled the .22 from his jeans and aimed it at Vito. "Only a fool surrenders all his weapons, old man. A dead fool."

"*Grande buono!*" Vito shouted, then leaned his head back and roared in laughter until he began to cough.

"This is why no one will ever forget that day. Why my men call you the *guerriero*. The warrior who is unafraid to bleed. It is true. You are the American Armanno."

Lucky had grown up with the story about how the *Cosa Nostra* had been born and why the words *this thing between us* had been chosen as the bond that would forever unite the fathers of Sicily. Dante Armanno had been one of those fathers. A young man in Palermo who had fought like a lion the day the French soldiers had invaded the city and killed his three sons and raped his daughters.

As much as Lucky rejected the idea that he and Vito were a lot alike, they had similar views on family and work ethic. He suspected it was why thirty years ago Vito had paid twice what Dante Armanno was worth—the American estate built in tribute to the legend—when it had gone to auction.

Unable to stay in the chair a minute longer without a drink in his hand, Lucky shoved himself to his feet. He was worth 2.4 million, and yet he wore what he always wore—jeans, leather boots and his seasoned leather jacket, a testimony to where he had been and what he had seen over the years in Chicago.

At the narrow mullioned windows, he returned his gun to his jeans. It had started to snow again. His thoughts briefly returned to the warm Florida sunshine he'd enjoyed a week ago. The sunshine and the sea witch—as he'd come to think of her.

He turned from the window. "Does Vincent D'Lano know that you have decided to replace Moody as your heir?"

"Not yet. But when he finds out—" Vito grinned "—he'll want to take a meat cleaver to both our necks. Since your brother rejected his daughter Sophia, Vincent has promised to tear down Masado Towers a brick at a time. I wonder what his threat will be once he learns you have stolen his ride to the top of the *famiglia.*"

"I have heard there are witnesses who are saying Vinnie masterminded my sister-in-law's kidnapping. If that's true, he'll be sitting in jail a long time." Lucky asked, "When you agreed that Moody would become your heir, did you ever speak to Vinnie about it? Or was it all arranged through Carlo?"

"Vincent came with Carlo once to gloat. But I never spoke to him or agreed to anything. Because I have no heir, Carlo decided I should turn over everything to his man of choice. A few weeks later in a letter, he warned me that if I took too long to die, he would have me carted off to a nursing home. It's true Vinnie will want what Carlo promised him, but it's not what I promised him."

"And if the changes in the will aren't what I requested and I decide to withdraw?" Lucky asked.

Vito pulled the will from his drawer. "It is done. My lawyer thinks a secret trust fund is suspect and I should demand to know whose name is on it, but I don't intend to."

Good, Lucky thought, because he had no intention of explaining his actions to anyone.

"I want the American Armanno as my heir. That is all I care about. That my men will be taken care of for their years of loyalty. I'm restocking the wine cellar with Macallan," Vito reminded him. "I've asked Summ to remove my things from the master bedroom so you can take control even before I die. I'm stepping down the minute your signature is on the papers. Tonight you will become CEO of Tandi Inc. and sole owner of Dante Armanno."

"I don't want your bed, old man."

"Since you have toured my house on your own, you're aware that the master bedroom has a warm-water pool. It will be of use to you when you start your recovery."

"My recovery?" Lucky's black eyebrows arched.

"I've had a discussion with your doctor. He's concerned about your continued delays in having the back surgery he recommended. He is afraid there may already be permanent nerve damage. As I said, I want the America Armanno as my heir, the toughest *soldato* in the city. But I wonder if that were tested today, if we would find it true."

Lucky never made promises he couldn't keep or claims that weren't within his power to guarantee. In truth, he knew he wasn't a hundred percent. Hadn't been for months.

"If your memory fails you, I will refresh it. Days ago I offered my assistance to you and your brother. Joey was able to rescue his wife from that bastard, Stud Williams, because of my generosity. For this you agreed to repay me with a favor of my choice. I have made my choice. You as my son. At least on paper."

A soft knock at the door sent Lucky back to the chair, licking his lips.

"Come in, Summ," Vito said. "I believe you met my housekeeper days ago."

When the door opened, a small Japanese woman entered the study with a bright blue parrot riding on her shoulder. Anxious for his requested Scotch, Lucky was disappointed to see the woman carrying a teapot and two stone cups on a bamboo tray.

"It looks like the wax in your ears is again causing

you a hearing problem, Summ," Vito grumbled. "We ordered Scotch, not tea."

"Hear fine. Drink Matcha tonight." Her gaze found Lucky. "Tea in honor of wise decision to become *wakai shujin.*"

"What did she call me?"

"Young master," Vito explained.

"*Gwaak!* Shoot the moron. Drop and roll! *Gwaak!*"

Lucky ducked as the parrot lifted off the woman's shoulder and sailed to a perch in the corner of the room.

"That would be Chansu," Vito explained. "He's part of Summ's ancestral family. A reincarnate, if you believe in that sort of thing. He and Summ come with the house."

The housekeeper placed the tray on the desk. She was a petite woman, dressed in green silk pants and a high-collared tunic to match. She looked mid-thirties, though Lucky knew she was older. For years there was talk that Vito had an Asian mistress.

She moved her long black plaited braid off her shoulder. Poured the tea. "Matcha good." Her eyes locked on Lucky. "You like."

No, he wouldn't, Lucky thought. Not if it tasted anything like it smelled. It reminded him of the stench that always clung to his neighbor's dog after he came back from a sewer run chasing rats.

Any minute he was sure Vito would set the housekeeper straight and send her out the door for the ordered Scotch. To his disappointment, it never happened.

While the woman poured the tea, Vito said, "I took the liberty of informing Summ about your medical problems. It looks like she's decided to aid your recovery in her own way. As you've already noticed, the tea smells like—"

"Roadkill," Lucky acknowledged.

Vito chuckled. "It tastes no better. But if you can get it down, it will ease your pain. Two years ago my doctors sent me home to die. They told me my throat cancer was too advanced. The next day Summ started brewing the Matcha." He accepted the cup of tea from his housekeeper. "After you sign the papers, we'll toast your future as the new master of Dante Armanno. Then, I'll tell you a story about your father. A story about the old days when Frank and I first became friends. Before he stole my wife and became my enemy."

The sheer curtains moved and Elena glanced at the open door leading to the veranda. A balmy breeze filtered in off the ocean, the surf making that familiar rushing noise her mother, Grace, loved so much, the one she claimed eased her pain and lulled her to sleep at night.

"What is it, Lannie? Have I been moaning again?"

Elena had been standing next to the white wicker bed for a long five minutes watching her mother sleep. "No, *Madre*," she said softly, leaning down to gently kiss Grace's forehead. "I just came to check on you."

Grace tried to raise her hand, but the attempt was met with an exhausted sigh.

"It's all right." Elena rescued her mother's hand and gently squeezed. "Everything is fine."

Four weeks ago Grace had suffered another stroke. It was the second in a year, the fifth in the past ten. The numerous strokes, the doctor explained, were caused from the accident her mother had incurred before Elena was born more than twenty years ago.

The accident had destroyed her mother's memory, along with her beauty. Elena couldn't remember a time during her childhood when Grace wasn't dealing with an excruciating headache or sleeping off the effects of a sedative to battle the daily pain she lived with.

"Your father brought me a new silk scarf. Ann helped me put it on. She doesn't do as nice a job as you do, Lannie, but she's getting the hang of it."

Ann was Grace's new live-in nurse. Elena eyed the lavender silk turban on her mother's head. "It matches your nightgown perfectly. From what I can see, I agree. Ann's attempt looks like she's improving. You look stunning."

Grace's eyes lit up. She loved compliments, even though she knew the scar that cut deep into her cheek had destroyed any chance of her being truly beautiful ever again. Still, the silk turbans she wore and the soft lingerie that draped her fifty-seven-year-old body salvaged a degree of her dignity.

Over the years Frank had gotten into a routine of sending monthly gifts in the mail when he was away. Grace's favorite had been the colorful silk scarves. To make them more usable, Elena had come up with the idea to fashion them into turbans to cover the numerous scars on her mother's head. Grace had loved the idea, and they'd had fun buying matching nightgowns and silk pant outfits to match the scarves.

"Your father retired from his job. Did he tell you?"

"He told me."

"I'm so happy."

In many ways Grace lived in a child's fairy tale. She had no idea where Frank had spent his time for the past twenty-four years, and Elena hadn't known, either. Until a few weeks ago.

"Rub my leg, would you, Lannie? It always feels so good. You have such magic in your hands."

Elena reached for a tissue from the bedside table and dabbed at Grace's mouth. One of the strokes had paralyzed her right side, and she rarely knew when she was drooling.

The muscles in her right leg had atrophied, as well. Despite Elena's concentrated efforts to slow the process down with massage therapy, the leg was shrinking.

She slid the hem up on her mother's nightgown and began to massage the shriveled limb.

"I'm glad you suggested that Frank learn how to do this for me. He's getting very good. He says he's going to take over the job so you can have more free time. Would you like that, Lannie? You could take a vacation with some of your friends."

"Maybe a short trip," Elena agreed, knowing she would be taking one very soon. But she wouldn't be going with friends.

"Guess what, Lannie? Frank says he's going to take me out in the boat. And guess what else? He says we can go every day if I get stronger."

"Then you need to eat," Elena reminded her.

"Guess what else? Frank says…"

Grace fell asleep with Frank's name on her lips. Twenty minutes later Elena left the room by way of the open door that led onto the sprawling oceanside villa's veranda. As she headed for the long stairway, Frank's voice stopped her.

"Elena."

She turned to find him standing in the shadows.

"Where are you going?"

"For a walk."

"It's late."

"I'll take one of the dogs with me." When that didn't seem to appease him, she added, "I'll ask Romano to accompany me."

"You've been very distant since I told you about Chicago and…my other life."

For years Elena had never questioned her father's extensive traveling or the guards that patrolled their ocean-side estate. She had believed that he was what he had claimed to be—a corporate salesman—and that the guards were just a cautionary measure because he was away so much. Days ago he'd revealed that he'd been living a double life, and that his true identity was not Frank Palazzo, but Frank Masado. His occupation: a capo in the Chicago Italian mafia.

Chin raised, Elena asked, "If Mother could remember her life before the accident, would she want to return to Chicago?"

The question brought Frank out of the shadows. He wore a white linen shirt and black pants, and with the black patch covering his right eye, he looked very much like the mobster he claimed to be.

"You said you were born in Chicago. Did my mother grow up there, too? Is that where you met her?"

"Your mother was born in Detroit. She had one brother. He, along with her parents, died in a car accident when she was twenty. But none of that is important now. It happened a long time ago."

"Mother's thrilled you've retired. Retired from your salesman position, that is. How long do you intend to keep that lie going?"

"There is no reason to tell her differently. I *am* retired, Elena. I can't go back to Chicago. I'm dead as far as the organization knows. Dead and buried at Rosewood Cemetery. For years I wanted to be here with you and your mother, but I didn't know how to make that happen. Not until my sons came up with a plan to fake my death."

"Oh, yes, my mystery brothers."

"I know that was a shock, Elena, learning that I had another family, but my life was not my own for many years. I did what I had to do to keep my family from being destroyed. Both families. My sons, and you and your mother."

Elena had been stunned when she'd first learned that Frank's other life included two adult sons, who were also a part of the mafia. On top of that, Frank had told her that there had been a contract put out on him.

"For your mother's sake, Elena, you must try to understand the situation. Accept it and forget it."

"I'm trying to understand. I just need more information for that to happen."

"Staging my death was a genius idea. I owe Joey and Lucky a great debt for finding me a way out. My sons were right. There was only one way out for me. I had to die in order to live."

Elena studied the man who, for twenty-four years, had allowed her to call him Father and believe it was true. She gazed at his ruggedly handsome face, then the black eye patch, and suddenly another piece of the puzzle fell into place. Rocked by the significance of her revelation, she brought her hand to her throat.

"What is it, Elena? What's wrong?"

"Your eye... Since I was little you've worn that patch. Oh, God! Is that it? Did someone in the organization do that to you? Did they hurt my mother, too?"

For years she had silently questioned her mother's so-called accident. By the look on Frank's face, she had been right to be suspicious.

"Mother didn't have an accident, did she? That's why you brought her here, isn't it? The reason for the guards? Why you became two people? You said it's complicated. Why is that? Is Mother supposed to be dead, too? And me? What kind of complication am I?"

She saw him stiffen, saw that he suddenly didn't know what to do with his big hands. He shifted his body, which put his face in shadow again. "I've told you what you need to know. What's important for you to know, Elena. The rest will only make you—"

"What? Afraid? Ask more questions? Questions like, who am I?"

He turned quickly. "You are Elena Donata Palazzo. My daughter. A beautiful young woman with a bright future ahead of her."

Elena played along. "And in this bright future will I have children?"

"Of course, if you wish."

"So if I have children, are you suggesting that I lie to them as you are lying to me right now?"

She watched his jaw clench.

"In other words, Frank," she went on, "who should I name when I tell my children who their grandfather is? You, the only father I have ever known? Or my real father, the man whose blood runs through my veins?"

His mouth moved, but no words came out. As if he

was paralyzed both in mind and body, he just stood there looking angry and formidable.

Only, Elena wasn't afraid. Frank might look capable of snapping her neck, but he had never shown an ounce of violence toward her. He hadn't even swatted her butt as a child when she'd deserved it.

"I know you're not my father," she said softly. "So don't try to placate me with another lie. I know my blood is not your blood. Unfortunately the records at the hospital don't list whose blood it is."

"Elena—"

"No." She held up her hand. "No more games."

"This was never a game."

Elena studied her father. No, not her father, the man who had posed as her father for twenty-four years. "You know who he is, don't you?"

"Elena, please."

"You know, don't you?" Against her best attempt to keep her emotions in check, Elena fought tears. "Tell me the truth! Do you know him?"

"Yes. I know him."

"But you're not going to tell me his name, are you? If you never wanted to play this game, end it now."

He shook his head. "*Non posso.*"

"You can't, or won't?"

"He doesn't know you exist. He can never know."

Tears on her cheeks, Elena started down the stairs.

"Elena!"

She didn't stop. Couldn't.

Frank followed her. "I was there the day you were born," he called out. "You are my daughter. Maybe not by blood, but I have loved you the same as I love my sons. Will forever love you as my daughter.''

Elena spun back around, the ocean breeze swirling her white skirt about her shapely calves. Tossing her midnight-black hair out of her eyes, she said, ''You should have told me years ago, Papa. I would have found a way to understand. You should have trusted me enough. Loved me enough!''

''Maybe you would have understood. Your real father would not have. And if your curiosity had led you to him…'' He shook his head. ''You're right, your mother is also dead in Chicago, as I am. That is what has kept her safe for twenty-four years. I'm sorry, Elena, but I couldn't tell you the truth years ago, and I still can't.''

# Chapter 2

After a week in an iron cell, Vincent D'Lano was twice as ornery as his reputation. "Listen, Martin, Carlo Talupa and I were in the middle of a deal worth billions. Do you think I would kill him before that happened?"

"This deal, will it still go through even though he's dead?"

Vincent shoved his stocky body out of his chair to pace the small room where he and his lawyer were meeting at the Cook County Jail. "Yes. If I can get my ass out of here."

"Then maybe you decided to kill Carlo and double your take."

The urge to strangle Martin English sent Vincent's hands into his pockets. If he killed his lawyer, he'd never get out of jail.

"I want out of this sewer, Martin. I want Sophia out, too. What are you doing about that?"

At fifty-eight, Martin English was not only a veteran

lawyer, but had worked for Vincent for fifteen years. Accustomed to his client's needs, as well as his temper, he said, "I might get you out within a week or ten days, Vince, but Sophia's going to have to be patient. The police have evidence that she hired two convicts in Joliet to break out Stud Williams. Unless we can make that evidence disappear, she may have to do some time."

"So get off your skinny ass and make the evidence disappear. Fix it, Martin, or I swear you'll look back on this year as the nightmare that never ended. Your wife won't just be crying at your funeral. *Capiche?*"

"These things take time, Vince. You've been named as an accessory to your daughter's crime. That—"

"You're not listening, Martin. Make it all go away. There are a dozen ways. Pick one. Do it. I was in the middle of a once-in-a-lifetime deal when this happened. And while I'm in here, Moody's running my affairs. Unchaperoned. You and I both know my son can't cross the street without pissing someone off."

Vincent had been a two-bit hood when he'd first met Carlo Talupa. But he'd been a smart hood, and he'd put too much time into his current plan to let his lawyer screw it up now.

He licked his lips as the image of Vito Tandi's impressive estate formed in his mind. He had admired Dante Armanno for years, but recently it had become a key element in his future.

Martin glanced at his Rolex. "I'm going to get kicked out of here soon. Before I go, I have a few more questions about your part in Stud Williams's breakout."

"I told you I had no part in that. Unfortunately. If Sophia had involved me, we wouldn't be in here."

"About these witnesses, Vince…"

"Make 'em disappear, Martin." When the lawyer just

sat there, Vincent came forward and slammed his fist
down on the cheap wooden table, his slicked-back gray
hair falling forward over his bushy black eyebrows.
"Sophia's only crime, Martin, was loving a man who
deceived her. I had a deal with Frank Masado. His son
was supposed to marry my daughter. But Joey rejected
her. What's she gonna do, Martin? Turn the other cheek?
She's a D'Lano. We've earned the right to demand respect."

"The court doesn't care about your sour deal with
Frank Masado, Vince. A crime was committed."

Vincent glared at his lawyer, who continued to sit
calmly in his silk suit and spin his diamond ring on his
index finger. "I won't be screwed over by this country's
dumb-ass judicial system."

With the agility of a man of twenty-five, instead of
sixty, Vincent D'Lano grabbed Martin by his suit lapels
and lifted him to his feet. Turning his index finger into
a toy gun, he pressed it to Martin's temple and knocked
off four shots. When he let go of him and stepped back,
the lawyer wilted back onto the chair, his complexion
turning as white as his shirt.

Pleased, Vincent said, "You know I don't make idle
threats, Martin. Get me and my daughter out of this
stinkhole, or your wife will be looking all over the city
for pieces of you to bury for the next ten years." He
patted Martin's pale cheek. "Crooked lawyers are a
dime a dozen. Don't disappoint me, Martin, or I'll kill
ya. I'll kill ya dead."

The exotic dancer was performing for Lucky as if he
was the only customer seated at the bar. Melody was her
name, and like all the other girls who entertained at the
Shedd, the diva had enough curves and sexy bump-and-

grind moves to give every man bellied up to the bar tight jeans and a fantasy to take home.

The catwalk where the dancers played tease-and-tickle with the customers ran between a double-sided bar, which allowed the bartenders to easily handle the crowd. Melody, who had been working Lucky for a long twenty minutes, finally gave up and wiggled her curves toward Moody Trafano a half-dozen barstools away. She bent over and shook her full breasts in Moody's grinning face, her efforts rewarded when he slid a twenty-dollar bill into her cleavage.

It had been two days since Lucky had signed Vito's papers, making him the new owner of Dante Armanno and CEO of Tandi Inc. The corporation was a conglomerate of various businesses throughout Chicago, and one of those businesses was the Shedd.

Tonight Lucky had come to the exotic bar to check out his property and to meet Jackson Ward. It was after ten, and Jacky was late. His friend hadn't been too excited about being called out this time of night. Lucky didn't blame him. Sunni Blais was one beautiful woman, and knowing Jackson the way he did, Jacky most likely had answered his cell phone in a prone position with his lovely fiancée snuggled next to him.

He glanced around the bar. Noted that the loud music and the near-naked dancers were keeping the bar packed and the men drinking. It was funny how fast things changed, Lucky mused. A month ago Milo was strutting through the Shedd playing big shot and now he was dead, and Vito had a new son—on paper, anyway.

He made eye contact with Melody. She smiled and gave him an I-know-how-to-make-you-feel-a-whole-lot-better look. That look reminded Lucky she was a professional off the catwalk, as well as on, and as the new owner of the establishment, getting to know what made each one of his employees tick wouldn't only be smart, it could be entertaining.

He finished his drink, deciding Melody would have to wait. Jackson would show soon. But maybe afterward he'd see if the dancer was still around.

His glass had been refilled for the third time when he saw *her*. He wasn't drunk, so he knew she wasn't a mirage. Still, he glanced down at the amber liquor in his glass, wondering if someone had slipped him a little surprise. But even as he considered it, his gaze went back to the shadowy entrance where the neon sign over the door was putting a rosy tint in Elena Palazzo's cheeks.

She looked left, then right. Scanned the bar. When their eyes met and locked, he watched her slip through the crowd, her shiny black hair moving around her slender shoulders.

She wasn't dressed to be noticed, but that didn't stop the men from taking a second look. She had an angel's face, and a walk that would make a man follow her to hell and back on his knees, dragging a dead horse. It was the combination of innocence and that walk that had kick started his own fantasies about her weeks ago.

He'd been around plenty of beautiful women over the years, but Grace's daughter had it all. Everything. Too much of everything, he decided as his gaze focused on her V-neck white fuzzy sweater and the damn fine job it did of framing her assets.

He raised his glass to his lips, his gaze shifting to where her sweater ended and her pants began. The pants were the color of caramel and rode low on her curvy hips. Low enough for every man to see the shiny gold ring in her navel.

It occurred to him as he glanced around the room that

every horny bastard in the place was anticipating Elena taking it all off on the catwalk; that she was assumed to be a dancer looking for a job.

Only they both knew she wasn't there to work the crowd. She was there to work…him.

She kept walking—no, floating was a better word— toward him, a lightweight black leather jacket tucked under her arm. Six feet away, she licked her full red lips and tossed her head. Two feet from him, she stopped and cleared her throat.

Then it came, the sexiest voice he'd ever heard—the one that had branded him from the moment they'd been formally introduced at Santa Palazzo two weeks ago. "In a bar with a drink in your hand. How original."

Lucky slid off the barstool, drained his third Scotch, then spun the empty glass back onto the bar. "What are you doing here?"

"We need to talk."

"You could have called. Both my number and Joey's are always with…" Lucky glanced around, rephrased what he'd been about to say. Frank was supposed to be dead. He couldn't very well claim that a dead man had his son's phone number. "You can reach me day and night at that number."

"Listen, you…you know why I didn't call. Here, or someplace private?"

"How did you know where to find me?"

She glanced at the empty glass. "It wasn't hard. My first stop was the Stardust at Masado Towers. When I didn't find you there, the bartender mentioned a few places not far from your house. I just happened to see this place—" she glanced at Melody "—and thought it looked like you." Her eyes found him once more. "You might say fate has dropped me in your lap."

Elena's sexy backside appeared in Lucky's mind, and he would have liked nothing better than her seated on his lap. Keeping his thoughts to himself, he asked, "Was it Jimmy at the Stardust who gave you my home address?"

"I already had your home address. I found it in the black book. Listen, you…" She took a step closer. "I'm not as *ingenuo* as I look, so let's stop playing games and get to it."

"That means what, exactly?"

"It means I didn't come all this way to count snow-flakes and share a drink with you in some sleazy bar. I'm here for the truth, and I'm sure you know what I'm talking about."

The bravado she was trying to sell him didn't match the way her hands nervously rubbed her slender thighs. He liked her hands, her small fingers and tiny unpainted nails. He also liked the fact that she didn't wear a lot of jewelry or a pound of makeup.

But then, she didn't need to. She was her mother's daughter. As beautiful as a midnight star and twice as bright. She was the sea witch, after all.

He shifted in hopes that the pain in his lower back would ease, and that the straining going on inside his jeans didn't accidentally move the safety off his .22 and blow him to hell and back.

He said, "You shouldn't be here."

"Here, as in here—" she eyed the men staring at her, then glanced at Melody again, who was now on all fours, her backside rolling with the music in a circular motion that had netted her several more green bills tucked into her G-string "—or are you talking about here, as in the big bad city of Chicago, where crime never sleeps?"

Without intending to, Lucky found himself grinning,

enjoying her wit as much as her sexy voice. But it was short-lived as Moody Trafano eased off his barstool and started toward them.

Like the other men, Moody had been watching Elena since she'd entered the bar. It was no secret that Trafano had a healthy appetite for pretty women, or that he spent more time on his back at the Shedd than sitting at the bar.

As he closed the distance, Lucky reached out and slid his arm around Elena's trim waist and hauled her into his space. "We're getting company," he whispered. "Be careful what you say. Don't get that pretty mouth of yours in trouble. Say nothing about who you are or why you're here."

Lucky's nose brushed her silky cheek, noting that her skin felt as soft and smooth as satin. He couldn't pinpoint her unusual scent, but he didn't need to name it to know he liked it.

She looked up at him with her catlike gold eyes just as Moody said, "You must be the new dancer we've all been expecting. My name's Moody Trafano, the soon-to-be owner of the Shedd. And you are?"

Elena held Lucky's gaze for a few seconds longer, then slowly turned around. She'd said she wasn't naive, but Lucky was sure she'd never dealt with a snake quite as slippery as Moody.

In a single glance Elena took Moody's measure, but didn't offer him her name. Good girl, Lucky thought. So far so good.

"You've got to be the most beautiful doll in this place," Moody complimented her. "And there's plenty here to compete with." His eyes left Elena's face to ogle the tanned swell of her breasts, then settled on her flat stomach and the gold ring in her navel. "How long have you been dancing?"

He raised his hand as if he couldn't control the urge to touch her a moment longer. Like a bulldog protecting his bone, Lucky grabbed Moody's wrist and squeezed. "I never share, Trafano. I never learned how. Get lost."

Moody wrenched his arm away. "She's the Shedd's property. That means she's anyone's fun if you got the bucks to spend, Masado. And I got plenty. Technically she's mine as soon as old man Tandi dies."

Lucky would have liked nothing better than to enlighten Moody on his recent deal with Vito and explain to him who actually owned the Shedd. He would have loved to watch Moody crap a brick in front of a full house when he heard he wasn't going to get a dime of Vito Tandi's fortune. Instead, he said, "The lady isn't a dancer, Trafano. Back off and have your fun with someone who likes snake oil."

"Lady?" Moody snorted. "This place don't get ladies in it." Eyes back on Elena, he said, "Sorry, doll, but facts are facts, right? And speaking of facts, a piece of information you'll appreciate is that Masado, here, is physically challenged. It's a known fact that drunks can't keep it up. I'm thinking maybe he can't even *get* it up anymore."

Normally Lucky would have driven the man's teeth down his throat for the insult, but he didn't feel like throwing any punches tonight.

Actually he hadn't felt like it in weeks, which was why he was going to let Moody's remark go by, instead of stomping on his throat and breaking his windpipe.

"What do you say you let me buy you a drink, sweet milk? I'm sure we can find a quiet place to talk. Better yet, how about taking a walk down the red carpet with me? You might as well get initiated by the best. And around here, I'm the best. The girls call me the Italian Stallion.''

Lucky felt Elena's hand slide between them, and before he believed she would do it, she had stolen his knife. A half second later the stiletto was touching Moody's jugular. "I've made my choice tonight, Mr. Stallion. Unless you want to be gelded right here, I suggest you trot on back to where you came from."

Her words sent a roar of laughter around the bar, and the color draining from Moody's face.

How Elena knew where she could find one of his knives was as much a mystery to Lucky as how she'd learned to wield it with such expertise. And by the look on Moody's face, he was wondering the same damn thing.

While the crowd continued to laugh and enjoy the show at Moody's expense, Lucky took hold of Elena's wrist and confiscated the stiletto. The blade back in his pocket, he stuck her to him like a postage stamp, spun her around and started to usher her toward the back rooms.

Before they reached the privacy of the hallway, Elena tried to wriggle out of his hold, but Lucky only squeezed her closer to him and said, "*Basta*, Elena. No more. We don't need another scene."

"I'm not afraid of that albino lizard," she spat. "He's a *parassita*. A sleazy *maiale*. A pig who—"

To shut her up, Lucky grabbed her around the waist and lifted her off her feet, so that she was dangling at his side. "If you're not going to shut up," he said, "I'm going to—"

"The last man who manhandled me, I spit in his face. Let go or I'll—"

She looked as if she was about to do as she'd warned. He swore, then planted his mouth over hers more to shock her into rethinking that move than anything else. He set her back on her feet a split second later and jerked her into step with him once more. "Walk, Elena, with your mouth shut," he warned. "Disgracing a man like Trafano in public isn't smart. Sexy sass a liquored-up man can handle. A woman sticking a knife up his nose he takes personally."

Lucky glanced over his shoulder to see that Moody hadn't moved, his angry eyes drilling Elena's back. His cheeks were no longer pale, but as red as Melody's spinning red nipple twizzlers.

Elena stopped trying to peel his fingers off her hip. And as he continued to escort her down the back hallway, the one covered in plush red carpet, she asked, "Where are you taking me?"

"Some place private."

She looked around, her gaze darting to the many doors lining the hallway. "Aren't these the rooms where…" She looked at him. "I thought we were going to talk."

"That's what I planned. You thinking something else?"

He glanced down and caught her glaring at him, the action drawing his attention to the golden flecks in her brown eyes. Had Frank known she wasn't his flesh and blood? Lucky wondered. Had he known from the beginning she wasn't his daughter? He had to have known the minute he'd seen her eyes.

She had her mother's straight little nose and full lips. Her mother's silky hair. But her eyes…she had her daddy's eyes.

Yes, he'd noticed her curvy body seconds before he'd noticed her sexy voice. But way before that, he'd noticed her eyes. The eyes that defied the lies and spoke the truth of who she really was.

"Where did you learn to handle a knife like that?" he asked, hoping conversation would keep his mind off how good she smelled and how much his .22 was cutting into his groin.

"A guard at Santa Palazzo. Romano Montel taught me all kinds of things."

I'll just bet he did, Lucky thought, instantly disliking the guard with a vengeance.

The bouncer that patrolled the hall tossed Lucky key number sixteen. "Palone called. He told me the news. Name's Blacky, boss. You need anything, you just let me know." The Shedd's troubleshooter eyed Elena. "You hire a new dancer?"

"No." Without further explanation, Lucky unlocked room number sixteen, shouldered the door open and spun Vito Tandi's daughter inside.

## Chapter 3

Apart from the sweet odor of Scotch that had trailed him out of the bar, Lucky Masado showed no outward signs that he was drunk. His speech was clear, and he'd walked in a fairly straight line down the hall.

Elena heard the door click shut, and before she turned around, she made a quick assessment of the no-frills room. It had definitely been designed to keep the customer's minds on what they were paying for. There was a small table and two chairs, and a double bed. Nothing else.

She was well aware that she was in a by-the-hour room and that her lips still tingled from a surprise kiss that wasn't really a kiss. Why she had taken the time to analyze what did or did not constitute the proper definition of a real kiss made no sense at all.

Yes, she had noticed Lucky Masado at Santa Palazzo; it was impossible to ignore a man whose reputation was as black as his hair. And yes, there was no disputing that he was handsome or that she'd found him interesting to watch. But then, so was a tropical storm, from a distance.

She slowly turned and found him leaning against the door with his arms crossed over his broad chest. He wore faded jeans and a light-colored shirt beneath a battered brown leather jacket. Pretty much the same clothes she'd seen him wearing when he'd visited Frank at Santa Palazzo two weeks ago, minus the jacket. He was tall, six-two, or maybe three.

He said, "You wanted to talk, Elena. Someplace private. Here we are."

She backed up until she felt the corner of the bed at her back. "You knew before we met that I wasn't your sister. How?"

"I flew to Santa Palazzo a little over a month ago on what you might call a witch hunt and ended up discovering you, along with Rhea and Niccolo."

"By spying on your father?"

"Yes."

"You invaded our privacy."

"Yes."

There was no apology in his husky voice. No regret in his brown eyes. He said, "You take morning walks along the beach. Sometimes as early as 5 a.m. You wear loose-fitting clothing the wind can play with. You take off your…shoes when you walk."

Elena's stomach knotted.

"When I discovered Rhea and Niccolo, I suspected the boy was my brother's son, but I had to be sure. I went to the hospital for proof. While I was there, I checked you out, too. That's the first I knew Grace was alive. That somehow my father had been able to get her out of Chicago years ago without anyone knowing it.

There was a rumor she was pregnant when she disappeared.''

Elena listened carefully to each word. ''And what did you do with the information?''

''Nothing. You weren't going anywhere that I could see, so I concentrated on Rhea and Niccolo. Joey had been searching for Rhea for three years. He had no idea Frank was hiding her in Florida or that she'd had his son. When Frank arrived in Chicago days later, I waited for your name to come up. When it did, Frank threw me a curve by claiming you were our sister. I knew it wasn't true, but I figured he had a reason for lying, so I kept quiet until I learned what it was. And you, Elena? How long have you known the sister story was a lie?''

''Not long.''

''Not long doesn't answer my question. When I was at Santa Palazzo and Frank introduced us, you knew then, didn't you? How long before that?''

''The night you and Joey came and took Nicci, Rhea was extremely upset. She had a right to be, but it was more than that. There were so many things I felt she wanted to say but couldn't. After she left Santa Palazzo to follow Nicci here, I decided to investigate a few things for myself. Like you, I ended up at the hospital several days later checking records and discovered Frank wasn't my real father.''

''But you didn't go straight to him with what you'd learned? Why?''

Elena tossed her coat on the bed. ''By then he was here in Chicago. Rhea had lived with us at Santa Palazzo for three years. She and I had grown close. I was concerned about her and Nicci. I wanted things to work out for them, so I decided to table what I knew until things settled down.''

"Frank was home almost a week before we arrived. You had five days to talk to him."

"And I was going to the night he returned. We sat down to talk and then he started telling me about his double life. About his sons, my half brothers. I knew it was a lie, the brother part, but I just listened." Elena shrugged. "I guess I was too confused at the time to question him."

The look Lucky gave her clearly called her a liar. "The truth is, Elena, you didn't trust him to tell you the truth. So you decided to make plans to find out the truth for yourself."

"It wasn't that easy. My mother is very dependent on me. I do things for her that no one else does. In order to leave Santa Palazzo to learn the truth, as you put it, I needed to teach Frank how to do those things. Since he's now *retired,* with no plans to ever leave Santa Palazzo, I spent the next week—" Elena paused "—I suppose you could call it, weaning Mother away from me."

"And he was willing to do these *things* for her?"

"I've never doubted Frank's love for my mother. Of course he didn't know I had an ulterior motive for suggesting that he get more involved in Mother's therapy now that he's home to stay. Tonight I gave him one more chance to tell me the truth. I told him I knew he wasn't my father. I asked him to give me my father's name. He refused, so here I am."

"Maybe he doesn't know who your father is."

Elena arched her delicate black eyebrows. "If you know, then Frank knows."

"Did I say I knew?"

"Come on, Lucky. Not you, too."

"Lucky? At Santa Palazzo it was Tomas. Out there—" he motioned to the other side of the door

"—it was, 'Listen, you.' What broke the ice? My charm in the hallway?"

There was no reason for him to bring up that stupid kiss, so why had he? And as far as his nickname went, she wasn't sure why she'd used it. But did it really matter? What was in a name?

Everything, she decided. After all, that was one of the reasons she'd come to Chicago.

Elena shoved away from the bed and gave him her back. The way he continued to take her apart with his dark eyes since they'd entered the room was starting to make her feel self-conscious. She had bought her outfit at the airport out of necessity. She hadn't thought about the weather until she'd gotten off the plane in her white summer skirt and sandals to twenty degrees and snow-flakes.

"You came to talk, Elena. So let's talk."

She turned back around and boldly studied him the way he'd been studying her for the past five minutes. He was taller and broader than his brother and father, but leaner.

Still, that wasn't what she'd noticed first about him—his drinking or his classic Italian nose. Or the visible scars on his hands and neck. What she'd noticed as she'd stepped onto the veranda at Santa Palazzo and laid eyes on Lucky Masado for the very first time was the rebel length of his midnight-black hair and how much of his soul she'd glimpsed in the depths of his brown eyes.

Again she focused on those soulful eyes, then on the way his sleek nose led her gaze straight to his rugged mouth and unshaven jaw. A second later she was appreciating the open V of his collarless muslin shirt and how it showed off his rich Sicilian skin and a smattering of black chest hair.

When she began to examine his beat-up leather jacket and the number of holes in it, she decided that they couldn't possibly be what they appeared to be or he would be dead, right?

Yes, he was his father's son. But even Frank, with his eye patch and all his intimidating ways, looked like a pussycat next to his street-soldier son with a rumored scar that ran more than half the length of his body.

Suddenly Elena needed to say it. To demand he give her what she'd come for. "Who is he, Lucky? Who is my father? I want his name."

"I can't tell you that, Elena."

Elena ignored the way her stomach did a slow flip. When he said her name, he dragged it out, reminding her of thick syrup fighting to stay in the bottle.

He angled his head just enough to give her a better view of the vivid scar that ran down the side of his neck and disappeared into his shirt. Was that the one? Elena wondered. Was that the beginning of the rumored scar that had almost killed him?

He unfolded his arms and shrugged off his leather jacket and dropped it on the floor. She watched the way he moved, ran her tongue over her teeth. Remembered the kiss that wasn't a kiss.

"You could be in danger if certain people in Chicago were to find out your identity, Elena. You're what is known as a loose end."

"A complication."

"Yes. Coming here and stirring things up is no good. Your father's name was not kept from you to hurt you, but to protect you. You and your mother."

"That's what Frank said, but I didn't—"

"Believe him? This isn't a game, Elena."

She stiffened, resenting that word more and more. "I

know that. I have no intention of broadcasting my identity to the world. All I want is his name. Give it to me, and I promise I'll be on the next flight back to Key West.''

''You think his name will be enough?''

''Yes.''

''I think you want the name to be enough.'' He shook his head. ''We both know it won't be.''

''I don't think you know me well enough to say that.''

''What I know is that Frank has successfully kept your mother alive for twenty-four years. Do you want that to change, Elena? Is a name worth jeopardizing her safety?''

''I love my mother. I don't want to hurt her. I want to understand. I want to know who I am. Why—''

''Why what?''

''Why it was kept from me.''

''You ask for something I can't give you. Only your mother has a right to tell you who your father is. Or Frank.''

''You know Mother can't tell me because she can't remember the past. And Frank won't. That leaves you.'' Frustrated, afraid she'd come all this way for nothing, Elena said, ''The saying goes, every man has his price. Since we both know you don't need money, what do you want for the name?''

''You don't have anything I want.''

''Are you sure about that?''

''*Sì.* I am sure.''

He shoved away from the wall and moved past her to the bed and picked up her jacket.

''I saw you,'' she said, watching him rifle the pockets.

Finding nothing, he tossed the jacket back on the bed, then glanced at her. ''Saw me where?''

"Hiding in the shadows outside the house at Santa Palazzo the night before you flew back here with Joey and Rhea. I knew it was you because I smelled the smoke from your cigarette." And the Scotch, Elena wanted to say, but she didn't. "And when I went for a walk along the beach, you followed me."

"Did you intend to swim?" he asked. "You brought a towel, but you never used it."

"Did you follow me hoping to see what you could see?" she asked boldly.

He smiled and it softened his hard mouth. "Maybe I followed you to protect you from the dark. Or from the ocean monsters who come out after midnight to watch the sea witch swim naked in the moonlight."

He had admitted to knowing her morning routine. What had made her think he hadn't followed her after dark, as well—more than once?

That realization sent Elena's stomach into another slow nervous flip—he'd seen her shed her clothes and *swim naked in the moonlight.*

"All right," Elena said softly. "Once more. Right here. I'll take off my clothes so you can get a closer look. Then afterward…for looking your fill, you'll give me my father's name."

She waited for his answer. Waited, and felt her cheeks come alive with embarrassment over the insane proposition she'd just offered him. She'd never done anything so utterly reckless in her life.

"You think all I want is to look? To see what I can see?"

Those words on his lips, as slow and liquid as her name, tripled the color in Elena's cheeks before moving down her throat.

He reached out and brushed the back of his hand

along her hot cheek. "It's generous of you to be willing to sacrifice so much for a name, but I'm going to have to pass on your offer."

When he started past her, Elena panicked and stepped into his path, again nearly knocked over by the sweet smell of liquor. "Okay, more. You can—" her face burned hotly "—touch me."

His expression never wavered as his gaze slowly traveled over her, seemingly assessing what he would get to touch. His eyes spent time appreciating the exposed swell of her breasts, then drifted to the gold ring in her navel.

Elena bit her lip, afraid he was going to again pass on her offer. Desperation was the only logical reason for the next thing that came out of her mouth. "Okay, everything, then. All of it. You can have—"

With lightning swiftness, he lifted her off her feet and tossed her onto the bed. Elena cried out, but that didn't stop him. The second her back hit the bed, he was straddling her and pinning her hips to the mattress with his stone-hard thighs. "I can have what, Elena? Are you going to spread you legs for me, too?"

The words sounded crude. More embarrassment flooded Elena's cheeks as she studied his clenched jaw and his angry black eyes. "I want my father's name," she whispered in an attempt to explain herself. A place to start, she thought silently.

His gaze settled on her breasts where they were straining the buttons of her sweater. While she struggled to breathe, he said, "I can get what you're offering any day of the week. Free of charge now that I own this place. And I'm sure the girls here are more experienced."

His insult fed Elena's bravado. "They should be," she reasoned. "I'm not a whore. I'm—"

His eyes lit on her face. "You're what?"

She clamped her mouth shut, closed her eyes to conceal the emotions storming her body, as well as her mind. She had never had a man on top of her before.

"Come on, Elena," he coaxed. "What are you? A virgin, maybe? A twenty-four-year-old virgin? No, I don't think so. Virgins don't swim naked and they don't sell their bodies for information."

She blinked open her eyes to argue the point and found him staring at her with a mocking grin on his face that made her feel cheap and dirty. Overcome with anger, she raised her hand and slapped his face. Hard.

For a moment there was nothing but silence while her handprint turned a vivid shade of red on his cheek, and in that space and time she became acutely aware of the heat growing between them. The sudden tightness drawing her nipples into hard peaks and the weakness in her limbs making her want to fidget.

"Get off me, Lucky. *Presente!*"

"You're a virgin?"

"Get off me."

"Answer me, dammit."

She heaved her body up to fight his weight. "Get off me!"

"Or what, Elena? What will you do, my hot-tempered little virgin?"

"Don't call me that," she snapped. "Get off me or I'll scream."

Instead of doing as she asked, he reached out, clamped his hands around her wrists and wrenched her arms over her head. Leaning forward, he said, "They're used to hearing screaming coming from these back rooms—

that's why the music is so loud. Go ahead, Elena, wear yourself out.''

She didn't scream, but she renewed her fight, twisting and wriggling while she began to curse him using every filthy word she knew in both English and Italian.

He shifted his body, and she suddenly felt more of him. Too much of him. She saw his jaw tighten. His nostrils flare. She stopped thrashing.

''I thought you were going to scream,'' he taunted. ''What are you waiting for?''

Above her head, he collected both of her wrists into one hand, then ran the fingers on his free hand down her throat and over the swell of her left breast. She sucked in her breath, shook her head. ''No! Lucky, please…''

''I'm going to ask you some questions, Elena. And you're going to answer them. Say, yes, Lucky, I'm going to answer your questions. All of them.''

His voice was soft, his breath eighty-proof. Could a person get drunk on fumes? Elena wondered. For she had to be drunk; why else would she have made him that stupid offer? Why else was she suddenly feeling like a cat needing to be stroked?

''Elena—''

''Yes, Lucky,'' she managed. ''I'm going to answer all of your questions.''

''Frank has no idea you're here, right?''

She swallowed hard, shook her head. ''I don't think so. He shouldn't discover I'm gone until around seven tomorrow morning.''

He slipped her top button out of its bound buttonhole. ''And then?''

''And then he'll find the note.''

His hands were warm on her flesh, torturously gentle.

His fingers moved to the second button. "The note says what?"

Intoxicated, yes—his breath was making her dizzy.

"What's in the note, Elena?"

She licked her lips, stared at his mouth. "I told him that I went to visit friends in Miami. College friends."

She felt his sweet breath touch her breasts and knew another button was lost. She tried not to think about it, about what he could see. About the fact that the bra she wore was pale blue and as sheer as fishnet.

"Mother suggested a vacation," she said. "I told Frank to tell her that I would call in a few days."

Another button.

Elena heard herself moan when his lips brushed her mouth. Oh, God... *"Piacere,"* she whispered.

"Please what, Elena?"

She closed her eyes. "Please...no more. Please stop."

Immediately his hand lifted off the fourth button, and she felt him draw himself upward. Though he remained straddling her, he let go of her wrists. In an ultrasoft voice, he demanded, "Open your eyes."

She blinked them open, fought to breathe.

"The lesson here, sweet Elena, is that I could take you with or without your consent. I could take... everything. All of it, as you say. I could hurt you. Scar you. Even kill you. Never play a game you can't win, Elena. And there are damn few you will ever win if you play with me."

His gaze dropped to the swell of her breasts, and Elena knew his interest centered on her puckered dark nipples. He stared at her for a few seconds longer, then he began to work the buttons back into the holes.

He was on the second button from the top when he let out a strangled groan—a sound of pure agony that stiffened his body like a knife had been driven into the middle of his back.

Elena watched as he wrenched hard to the right and rolled off her. A second later he was sprawled beside her on his back, his expression fighting an invisible pain.

Lucky recognized the rush of pain and knew what it meant. Flattened out on the bed, he gritted his teeth against the burning sensation racing the length of his spine, and the knowledge of what the outcome would be in a matter of seconds.

Not now, he thought, not the hell now. Not here and not in front of her.

He continued to lie there while the hot pain worked its way into his thighs, then began to melt away, taking with it the feeling in his limbs.

"What is it?"

Sweat beading his forehead, Lucky glanced at Elena. She was sitting up and staring down at him. He would have liked to have been sitting up, too. But without looking like a snake dragging a fifty-pound ball and chain, he wasn't going to be able to haul his body up.

"What's happening?" She slid off the bed. "It's your back, isn't it? Something happened to your back."

"What do you know about my back?"

She stepped between his open legs where they hung limp off the bed. "I heard Joey talking to Frank about some kind of surgery you're supposed to have."

"You just happened to hear?"

"All right, I was eavesdropping. And why shouldn't I? In a matter of weeks I learned that my father who isn't really my father is living a double life. Has two grown sons. And that they all work for the mafia."

"We don't work for the mafia, Elena."

"Sorry. You are the mafia."

Not liking that definition any better, Lucky checked his watch. The paralysis he'd been experiencing for the past three weeks was erratic. He could be up and moving within ten minutes or down and out for an hour.

"I take it this has happened before. You don't look too surprised."

No, he wasn't surprised. His doctor had warned him that the scar tissue from his old wound had begun to strangle his spinal cord. Internal adhesions—those were the words used—were constricting the blood flow. He'd had a few problems with the scar over the years. But it had gotten a helluva lot worse since Milo's boys had worked him over a few months ago and he'd wound up in the hospital losing a kidney.

"Should I call someone?"

"No."

She reached out and pulled his shirt from his jeans. When she began to unbutton it, he grabbed one of her wrists. "What do you think you're doing?"

"I'm going to check out the problem to see what I can do to help."

He shoved her hand away. "What you can do to help is go back home."

"You can't feel your legs, can you?"

He looked down to see that she'd curled her hands around his legs just above his knees and that she was squeezing. He knew that because he could see it, not because he could feel it. "Of course I can feel my legs."

Her hand moved to his front pocket.

"What the hell are you doing now?"

"I'm getting your knife so I can stab you in the leg. I wager a thousand that you won't feel it go in or out."

Lucky grabbed her wrist again. "Go sit over there."

She tucked a black strand of hair behind her ear. "And if I don't, what will you do? Get up and make me?"

He let go of her wrist and drilled her with a look that normally sent his men running for cover, but it didn't move her back even an inch.

"That's what I thought." She shook her head, reached out and resumed unbuttoning his shirt.

This time, as her fingers brushed his bare chest, Lucky closed his eyes and allowed himself the pleasure of actually feeling her hands on him. A minute later he felt cool air on his chest and knew she'd finished the task.

Angry all of a sudden that he'd succumbed to her so easily, he said, "Anxious to get rid of your little problem, are you?"

"My problem?"

"Your virginal status," he clarified.

"Years ago it would have been considered a gift. But I suppose these days the real gift to the modern man is variety and experience." She glanced at his legs. "It looks like I'm stuck with my problem, and you're stuck with yours. I wonder which is worse—inexperience or inadequacy."

Lucky reached out and grabbed her arms, then jerked her forward onto his body. "My legs are useless at the moment, but everything else is working fine. Am I right?"

Her sweet mouth parted, and she sucked in a breath of air. "*Sì, ho capito.* Now let me up. You've proved you're still…capable," she managed.

"If you're willing to do a little of the work, I could show you just how capable, Elena. We could start working on that experience you lack."

She squirmed, tried to roll off him, the friction only

adding more fuel to his capability. He closed his eyes, hoping that would help take his mind off what her body was doing to him, but her sexy scent filled his nostrils, and the result was another inch.

"Lucky…"

Her voice told him she was aware of what had just occurred. He let go of her, knowing he was making himself suffer needlessly. He had no intention of sleeping with Vito Tandi's daughter. He might want to, but he wouldn't. Temptation was a fool's game, and everybody in Chicago knew Lucky Masado was no fool.

# Chapter 4

*The rules on sex, dating and men are as follows, Lannie. Don't ever let your body rule your head. Don't say yes when you mean no. And never let a man get you cornered or down. Down as in off your feet and on your back. If it happens, Lannie, be prepared to feel the snake come alive. Am I making myself clear, darling? If you feel the snake, you're in trouble and you must knee the beast and run. Run like hell, Lannie. That is, unless you want to be caught. You'll want to be caught one day, darling. All women do. But we'll talk about that when you're older. For now I'll ask Romano to teach you some self-defense.*

Her mother's words had been offered to her when she was twelve, and Elena had gotten several more lessons on sex, dating and men in the years that followed. And defense lessons from Romano.

Elena stood between Lucky's legs, aware that what she'd felt moments ago had been the snake. Her gaze drifted to the front of his jeans. Not thinking too clearly, she asked, "Does this happen often? You know—" her eyes darted to his face "—ah, your back locking up and your legs going limp. I mean, numb."

She focused on the vivid scar that curled around his hipbone just above his jeans. It had to be the one, she thought. The legendary scar that went on forever. Did it go up or down? If it went up, it likely climbed his back to merge with the scar on his neck.

Accustomed to touching people in her line of work, Elena reached out and ran her finger across the visible five inches of the questionable scar. "I went to school at a medical institute for myofascial therapy. My interest, in the beginning, was just to help my mother with her pain." When he said nothing, she continued to carefully examine the portion of the scar she could see.

Her professor at the college had told her that her personal experience with her mother had given her compassion, as well as the dedication needed to become an effective therapist.

She asked, "When you lose the feeling in your legs, how long does it last?"

He didn't answer, which told Elena that he was either being stubborn for pride's sake, or that the paralysis was still in an inconsistent state.

She continued to study the thick fibrotic tissue, pressing into the scar with her thumb, adding more pressure as she moved it over the scar with immeasurable slowness.

On an intake of breath, he grumbled, "Go ask Blacky for a bottle of Scotch."

She kept her eyes on her fingers as she examined the scar. "You don't need more to drink. What you need is—"

"Scotch, Elena."

His tone was razor sharp and she looked up.

"Two bottles." When she still hesitated, his nostrils flared. "Now!"

Elena backed away from him and left the room. She found Blacky standing at the end of the red carpet enjoying the show on the catwalk. This time the half-naked woman was a six-foot redhead with breasts the size of Florida grapefruits.

She quickly instructed him to bring two bottles of Scotch to number sixteen, and when she returned to the room, she saw that Lucky had pulled himself up against the headboard.

"Blacky's on his way with your order," she said tightly. "What else will you be needing besides a new liver and a breath mint?"

"You."

"Me?"

"*Sì.* Come here, Elena. Come push one of these pillows behind me so I can sit up straighter. I'm helpless, remember?"

"As helpless as a viper, you mean."

His gaze drifted over her, slowly and deliberately. "Come here."

She did what he asked. Rounded the bed and climbed onto the mattress. In the process of shoving a pillow behind him, a hard rap sounded at the door. It was the only warning they got before the door opened.

Elena looked up expecting to see Blacky, then gasped when Moody Trafano walked into the room wearing his lizard's grin and carrying Lucky's two bottles of Scotch.

This just wasn't his night, Lucky decided as Moody Trafano kick the door shut. "Where's Blacky?" he inquired, knowing the answer before he asked the question.

"Taking a nap in number five." Moody's gaze locked on Elena. "You should have been nicer to me at the bar, doll."

Lucky tried to move his legs, but even as he worked at the hopeless cause, he saw Moody's grin grow wide. The bastard had already guessed why he was still sprawled on the bed, instead of on his feet.

"I thought it was all talk, you becoming a cripple. Guess there's a reason for you drinking a case of Scotch a day, after all." Moody's smile shifted to Elena where she sat on her knees on the bed. "You scared yet, doll? You should be. I don't like mouthy women unless they're on their knees." He chuckled at his own joke.

"You don't want to do this, Trafano," Lucky warned. "I'll have to kill you if you touch her. Kill you slow. *Capiche?*"

"Maybe I'll just have to kill you first." Moody set one of the bottles of Scotch on the table. Opened the other one. Motioning to Elena, he said, "Unbutton your sweater and come here. I want to look at you."

Instead of doing as she was told, Elena rebuttoned the top two buttons on her sweater.

"What's the matter? Not as mouthy without a knife, doll?" Moody tipped up the bottle, took several swallows. "It's too late for regrets, sweet milk. You should have given me the respect I deserve."

"You don't know what the word means," Elena replied.

Moody raised the bottle to his lips again and drank deeply. Wiping his mouth on the back of his hand, he set the bottle on the table. Then he pulled his dark green sweater off over his head to reveal a clean-shaven muscular chest. He flexed his biceps. "Come on now, doll. We both know you're not shy, so bring that sweet ass of yours over here."

Reaching for the bottle, Moody pulled a chair away from the table and placed it in the middle of the room. Taking a seat on it, he tipped his head back and chugged more liquor.

"Don't get off the bed, Elena," Lucky whispered. "Stay where you are."

"And that's going to help us in what way?" She whispered back. "Maybe if I pretend to like him, I can—"

Lucky gripped her wrist. "Don't leave my side."

"You can't move, remember?" She twisted her wrist free.

"Do as I say, Elena."

"Give me your knife," she suddenly suggested. "The Hibben, not the Haug. I've never liked how that style handle fits my hand."

Her words brought his head around, his eyes searching hers. "How do you know what I'm carrying or the difference between…"

His thought process shifted when he felt her hand on his hip. Remembering how quickly she'd stolen his knife at the bar, Lucky covered her hand with his, then curled his fingers around hers and slowly squeezed. If he wanted to, he could break her fingers one by one. "I'll handle this," he mouthed at her.

She mouthed back, "Without legs? I don't think so."

Moody finally came up for air after he'd drained half the bottle. "Damn, that's good Scotch."

He licked his thin lips, studied the last two inches in the bottle. As he tipped his head back to drain what was left, Lucky slid his hand to the front of his jeans and unzipped himself.

"What are you doing?" Elena whispered.

"Handling it," was Lucky's answer as he slid his hand into the opening to palm the .22 tucked next to his groin. Then, easing the weapon out through his open fly, he aimed it at Moody Trafano's kneecap and pulled the trigger.

Elena fidgeted in the back seat of a cold taxicab. The aging Buick sat idling nosily under a lamppost behind the Shedd.

Thirty minutes ago she'd been escorted out the back entrance into the alley by Blacky—who was wearing an angry purple welt on his forehead. There, he had placed her in the cab and told her to sit tight.

The image of Lucky's hand going into his jeans by way of his zipper and coming out with a gun flashed behind Elena's eyes. What followed was Moody Trafano screaming in pain as he toppled off the chair clutching his shattered knee.

She'd never witnessed a man being shot before. The blast had made her ears ring and she'd felt physically sick. Dazed, she'd been unable to move as the door had flown open seconds later and a man brandishing a .38 had charged inside demanding, "Dammit, Lucky, what the hell's going on in here?"

She had learned minutes later that the man was a cop, as well as Lucky's friend. Jackson Ward was as tall and dark as Lucky, with a heavy-hitter voice and an aggressive nature. In short order, he'd looked over the situation, sworn when he locked eyes on the smoking gun in Lucky's hand, then promptly went to work.

In mop-up mode, he had flashed his badge at a number

of curious employees and customers who had collected in the hallway, establishing himself as the one in control of the situation. After that, he'd handled everything with the efficiency of an army general while Lucky had continued to lie on the bed.

Moments ago a van had pulled into the alley and Blacky had carried Moody Trafano out and loaded him into it. Elena imagined that he would be taken to the hospital. Either that or…

No, if Lucky had wanted him dead, he would have killed him, instead of wounding him. There had been no hesitation or indecision as he'd aimed and pulled the trigger.

Elena laced her fingers together and worked at peeling another layer of skin off her lower lip. It felt raw and it stung, and yet she had continued to nervously pull off layer after layer.

She sighed, glanced at the back of the cabbie's head, then at the people who passed by on their way to wherever they were going at one in the morning.

Lucky carried a loaded gun between his legs. The reality again sent Elena's heart racing. What kind of man did something like that?

As if the silent question summoned the man himself, Lucky stepped out the back entrance of the Shedd into the blowing snow smoking a cigarette. He was walking on his own power, moving as if nothing was wrong with him.

Her gaze drifted…settled on his crotch. Was it there? Was the deadly little .22 there inside his jeans?

Jackson Ward came through the door seconds later. Dressed in jeans and a leather jacket similar to Lucky's minus the bullet holes—yes, Elena now believed that was exactly what they were. Jackson stopped beneath

the street lamp to exchange a few words with Lucky,
then climbed into the van with Moody Trafano.

When the van drove away, Lucky's gaze shifted to
the taxicab as he continued to smoke his cigarette underneath the street lamp, blowing smoke into the crisp
cold air. A full minute later, or maybe two, he started
forward, his cigarette hanging out of his mouth with a
casualness that said he'd been at it a long time.

Elena watched him close the distance, ripping another
layer of skin off her lip. He tossed the cigarette before
opening the back door of the cab. Climbing inside, he
brought with him the renewed scent of Scotch and a blast
of cold air.

She shivered, scooted along the leather seat to give
him room. Her coat wasn't meant for winter weather,
and she burrowed into the seat, wishing she'd taken the
time to buy something more substantial.

"Paulie, let's go," he said to the cabbie.

Elena wondered if they were friends, or if Lucky knew
all the cab drivers in the city.

As they swung into the traffic, she asked, "Where are
we going?"

"Home."

She had been looking straight ahead. Now she
snapped her head around and looked at him in the dark
of the back seat. "Home? I'm not going back to Santa
Palazzo without—"

"My home."

"Oh."

A horn honked as Paulie floored the cab and crossed
lanes, then turned right at the next corner. The sharp turn
sent Elena leaning into Lucky. She jerked herself back,
but not before their eyes locked.

She quickly angled her head to stare out the window.

"So now you're afraid of me," he said. "Is that it?"

She looked back at him, the smell of liquor drifting up between them—that noxious sweet odor that couldn't be ignored no matter how hard she tried. "No. You were protecting me. *Grazie.*"

It was clear why he drank. But alcohol wasn't going to fix his back. It might dull the pain he was experiencing temporarily. But eventually he was going to have to address whatever was causing the paralysis.

Her gaze drifted to his legs and she tried to imagine him in a wheelchair. The thought made her shiver, and she hugged herself.

He must have noticed because he said, "Paulie, turn up the heat."

"You got it, Mr. Masado."

The heater made a high-pitched buzzing noise as it sent a blast of warm air into the back seat. It was followed by a ringing sound that had Lucky sliding his hand into the inside lining of his jacket to retrieve his cell phone.

Flipping the phone open, he said, "Talk fast, I'm busy. Palone… Now? Do you know what time it is? *Non posso.* I'm busy at the moment. Why not tomorrow? All right, dammit! Tell him, yes. I'll be there." After he'd pocketed the phone, he said to the cab driver, "Take the next exit, Paulie, and head north. There's been a change in plans."

Lucky hated the idea of taking Elena with him, but he couldn't very well leave her somewhere alone. And if he dropped her off at Joey and Rhea's penthouse, he would have to explain what she was doing in Chicago.

For weeks he'd intended to tell his brother the truth—that Elena wasn't their sister. But he'd put it off, looking for the right time. It would take some extensive explaining, and at the moment he didn't have a couple of hours to untangle the lies and make sense of the whole complicated story to Joey's satisfaction.

"Punch it, *amico*. Dante Armanno in ten minutes."

"Ten," Paulie promised, then pressed the accelerator.

"How is Rosa and your boy?" Lucky asked, trying to take his mind off the woman beside him.

"Fine now that Tito has come home. He is doing much better, too."

Lucky dug into his coat pocket and pulled out a card and dropped it over the seat. "Tell Tito to call me if he's looking to earn some money. I have a job for him if he's interested."

"*Grazie*. Rosa bake you her special focaccia. You know she is a good cook." Grinning ear to ear, Paulie floored the gas pedal the minute he pulled onto the Kennedy Expressway.

Lucky glanced at Elena, who was trying hard not to look at him. He knew the incident with Trafano had shaken her. At Santa Palazzo she was used to a quiet sheltered life. Though not too sheltered, he reminded himself, recalling how she'd handled his stiletto in the bar.

A virgin with a fetish for knives. Now that was a scary thought.

"Where are we going now?"

He glanced at her. "I have an unscheduled stop to make. You'll wait in the cab."

"And then?"

"Then I'm taking you to my place."

"And then?"

"We catch a few hours' sleep before I fly you back to Santa Palazzo."

She lifted her chin. "I'm not going anywhere with-out—"

"*Basta,* Elena. Coming here was a mistake. Frank will be pacing and chewing heads off until you're back and safe."

"Frank has no say over me any longer. He's not my father. If you force me to go back, I'll just run away again."

"I don't think so."

He liked the way she didn't back down to him. Liked the fact that she had been willing to go up against Moody, even though she would have been no match for him. There had been no tears and no begging for mercy. He had liked that, too.

No, Elena Tandi had too much of her father in her to beg, Lucky decided. She was definitely her father's daughter.

He reached out and ran his finger over her lower lip. "Hungry?"

"No. The lip thing is a nasty habit. You know about nasty habits, right? Sometimes you just do it without thinking. Kind of reminds me of your habit. Only, unlike drinking to excess, chewing on my lip won't eventually kill me. So who was that on the phone? Who's Palone?"

"No one." Lucky glanced outside and realized that the cabbie had managed to get him to Dante Armanno in record time. As he pulled up to the gate, he said, "Give me a minute, Paulie."

When the guard saw who climbed out of the cab, he said, "Palone said to expect you." He flashed a light into the back seat of the car. "He didn't say anyone would be with you, though."

"That's because I never told him," Lucky countered. The guard smiled, pressed the remote that opened the gate while Lucky climbed back in the car and instructed Paulie to drive through. "There will be another one a half mile up the road," he said.

Once inside the last gate, they rounded the circle driveway and parked in view of the statue of Armanno. To Elena, he said, "Don't leave the cab. This place is crawling with guard dogs. I shouldn't be too long."

Paulie said, "I've never been here. Is it true that Vito Tandi is the richest man in the city?"

"He was yesterday, Paulie. But the crazy thing about money is—" Lucky glanced at Elena "—like women, it can be here one day and gone the next. A man is a fool if he takes either one too seriously." He reached out and squeezed Paulie's shoulder. "Keep the car running so our passenger stays warm. It's worth an extra hundred to you and a new dress for Rosa."

Summ was waiting for Lucky when he stepped into the foyer. After giving him a humble bow, she led him in the opposite direction from the study. Over her shoulder, she said, "Your room ready now. *Shujin* say you move in soon."

Lucky had never agreed to move into Dante Armanno at all. Certainly not while Vito was still alive. But he said nothing to the housekeeper, just followed her to the room on the ground floor where Vito now slept.

When he entered the room, Summ did not follow him. He found Vito propped against a stack of pillows with his eyes closed, his metal walker within reach. His breathing was ragged and his face was gray.

Lucky cleared his throat, and the noise brought Vito's eyes blinking open. When the old man saw who was there, he said, "*Grazie,* my son. It is good to see you."

He coughed and blood surfaced on his lips. "As you can see, today I'm a little under the weather."

Lucky reached for a tissue on the bedstand and handed it to the dying capo. "What did you want to see me about?"

"I told you when you signed the papers that I was stepping down. You need to be here now to take over my affairs. I no longer have the strength to manage them."

"That's why you called me over here this late at night?"

"I expected you to move in yesterday. What do I have to do to get you here? Burn down your home in the old neighborhood?"

His weak grin told Lucky the old man had no plans to do what he threatened.

His grin faded as quickly as it had appeared. "I need to tell you something. Something I should have told you the other night."

Lucky removed his jacket and dropped it on a bench at the foot of the bed. "I can't stay long. You have ten minutes."

"Bring a chair and sit."

Lucky moved the metal walker and pulled a chair close to the bed. Seated, he asked, "So what couldn't wait until tomorrow?"

"In a matter of weeks, maybe days, I will be gone. I have no way of knowing when. Before it's too late I wanted to tell you that I gave the order for Stud Williams to be killed. He shot Milo weeks ago, and for that I hired someone to sabotage the car that was taking him back to Joliet. I would be lying if I said it wasn't personal, my killing him. It was very personal."

Lucky had determined that the accident that had

claimed Stud Williams's life a week ago hadn't been an accident.

"I also wanted to tell you what happened at Vincent D'Lano's cabin years ago."

Lucky thought it ironic that Vito had chosen tonight of all nights to discuss Grace while his daughter was outside waiting in the car—a daughter he had no idea existed. For time's sake, and because he had already heard the story from Frank, he said, "I know what happened."

"Frank's version. But he was unconscious for several hours. He told you what he thinks happened. Not what actually happened. There has been much speculation about who killed my wife that night. I know the rumors claim it was me. For the record, Lucky, I never killed Grace. I loved my wife. Even after I learned she'd betrayed me with your father, I still loved her. I could not hurt her."

"But she was hurt," Lucky said, knowing that the extent of Grace's injuries had drastically affected her quality of life.

"I tried to stop them that night, Carlo and Vincent, but they were like hungry animals on a blood scent. I tried to save my Grace, but Carlo had other plans." He coughed again and Lucky saw more blood in the tissue. "The police are looking for Carlo's murderer. Tell Jackson Ward to look no further. When the time comes and I am gone, go to my safe in the study. There you will find Carlo's watch and his gold ring. I took them off his body after I personally shot his head full of lead."

Not surprised, Lucky nodded.

"It felt good to kill him. He was the one who ordered Vincent to beat Grace and cut her lovely face. For years I have lived behind these walls in pain and shame. Before it is too late, I must right the wrong. That's why Vincent D'Lano must also die. He must pay as Carlo paid. But I fear I have waited too long to avenge my Grace. Vincent is still in jail, and I grow weaker every day.'' Vito reached out and gripped Lucky's hand. ''If I die before I can kill him, you must do it. You are my heir, and my enemies are now your enemies. My responsibilities, your responsibilities. Promise me you will kill Vincent D'Lano for me if I die before it is done, Lucky. Say you will kill the animal who destroyed my beautiful Grace, and took her from this world. From me…and your father.''

His energy spent, Vito slumped back against the pillows and closed his eyes while Lucky sat there mulling over what he'd just learned. So it was Vinnie who had tortured Grace, not Carlo.

He didn't know how long he sat there. Longer than ten minutes. The door opening jarred him. Summ entered, saying, ''He will rest now. If he has told you what is in his heart, then he is finally at peace. His journey will begin soon.''

# Chapter 5

Elena watched Paulie's head fall back against the seat for a second time. She waited another long minute, then eased open the cab door watching him as she did so. When he didn't move, she climbed out and closed the door quietly.

The night air was bitterly cold, and she shivered as she stepped away from the car and disappeared into the shadow of a tall tree. A line of shrubs wrapped the house. She avoided the front entrance and found an unlocked iron gate on the west side of the house. She slipped through it, aware that she could meet a guard dog at any minute.

She had experience with befriending guard dogs, but nonetheless, she hurried up the paved path. She had no idea why she'd gotten out of the cab. It was as if an unexplained force had pulled her from the cab, and that same force was challenging her to enter the house.

The estate was guarded much like Santa Palazzo.

Only, there were more guards, and from the sound of it, more dogs, too. She could hear them now. They'd picked up her scent. Sure they'd be upon her in a matter of seconds, Elena scrambled toward a heavy glass-and-iron door. She pulled a lock pick from inside her boot and worked quickly to open the door. She hurried into the house and closed the door just as two large Rottweilers pressed their noises to the glass and showed their teeth. The corridor was dark, and the smell of lemon oil and cloves melted around her as Elena stared at the grandeur of polished wood and a mammoth crystal chandelier hanging from a vaulted ceiling.

She kept her ears attuned to the slightest noise, but the house was as quiet as a tomb. The spacious corridor fed into three separate hallways. She selected the right and soon found herself moving past a stairway and a massive clock that stood at least eight feet tall outside an archway into a large living room. She peeked inside the room and found a fire glowing in a huge stone hearth. The room was full of rich leather furnishings.

She moved down another hallway, this one lined with gold-framed shadow boxes filled with old guns and ancient swords. Suddenly she heard voices. Afraid of being discovered, Elena hurried toward the first door she came to and disappeared inside. Holding her breath, she listened as the voices grew louder, then receded, along with their footsteps.

She let out a relieved sigh, then turned. She was in the study, she surmised. Bookshelves lined one wall, and a worn leather chair sat behind a sprawling desk. There was a lit green banker's lamp on the desk, and the smell of lemon and cloves had been traded for aromatic tobacco. A pristine red velvet sofa sat along one wall and a single matching chair in front of the desk. Both looked rarely used.

When she spied the wooden bird perch in the corner, she took a second look, one black eyebrow hiking with curiosity. A few seconds later, her gaze moved to the picture on the wall directly above the perch.

For the next several seconds Elena forgot to breathe, her gaze locked on the gold-framed portrait. A portrait of a smiling young woman in her late twenties. A beautiful black-haired woman Elena easily recognized.

On a strangled sob, she gasped, "Mother?"

Lucky swore, then slammed the cab door shut. Elena was gone, and Paulie—who admitted sheepishly that he'd dozed off—hadn't seen her leave the cab.

The devil was definitely out to get him tonight, he thought as he paid Paulie and sent him back to town.

Returning to the house, he located Benito Palone. "I had a woman in the car with me when I got here. She's not there any longer." He frowned, the words spoken out loud irritating the hell out of him all over again. "Find her and bring her to me. Unharmed. Someone had to have seen her."

"Yes, sir. We'll find your woman."

"She's not my woman," Lucky said. "She's... Never mind. Just find her." Benito was halfway down the hall when Lucky called him back. "Do you carry a cell phone?"

"Yes."

Lucky pulled his own from his pocket. "Let me program the number. If I want to reach you, I don't want to have to waste time running you down. And likewise the minute you find Elena, I want to be called. She's five-seven, has black hair to her shoulders. She's wearing brown pants and a short black leather jacket. She has the face of a angel, but don't underestimate her. And watch your pockets. She likes sharp knives.''

It took no more than a few seconds to program the number into the cell phone, and then Benito hurried off to turn Dante Armanno upside down in search of Lucky's woman.

Anxious, and not willing to just leave Elena to Palone and the guards, Lucky headed out the back door. But after an hour had passed, and Elena was still nowhere to be found, he returned to the house more worried than angry. It was as he was heading down the hall, contemplating searching the house from top to bottom, that he heard a noise coming from Vito's study.

Confused how Elena could have managed to breech the house security, he entered the study and found her seated behind Vito's desk—the surface scattered with papers and a number of photo albums.

The minute he saw her pale face in the lamplight, he knew that her search for her father's identity was over. He was rarely careless. But tonight he'd made a major mistake. A mistake he might live to regret. "Elena?"

She looked up, wiped the evidence of tears from her cheeks. When her eyes shifted to the portrait on the wall of her mother, Lucky's gaze followed. Grace could be Elena's twin—except for the eyes.

"She was beautiful." She looked down at the pictures covering the desk. "She's smiling in all of these pictures." She gazed up at him. "So what changed all that, Lucky? What happened to my mother while she was married to Vito Tandi?"

It was as she stood that Lucky saw the blood on her hand. "What happened?"

"Broken glass," she explained. "I wanted to see if

the wedding picture was dated.'' She stepped away from the desk. ''It wasn't.''

''How bad are you hurt? Let me see, Elena.''

''It's just a scratch.''

Not trusting her definition of the word *scratch*, he flipped open his cell phone, suddenly remembering that Palone still had the guards out searching the grounds. Speaking quickly, he explained that he had found Elena and that he needed Palone's assistance in Vito's study pronto.

When he advanced on her, she stepped away. ''Elena, let me have a look at your hand.''

''I told you it's nothing.''

Her voice shook and she cleared it twice. She'd been lied to for years. Lucky had no idea what that felt like. Wouldn't begin to presume what she was feeling at the moment.

Minutes later Palone stepped inside the study and asked, ''Where did you find her?''

''In here.''

Palone frowned. ''How did she get into the house?''

''I came in the side door,'' Elena offered. ''It was unlocked.''

''That's impossible.'' Palone glanced at Elena, then the picture of Grace. Lucky watched as recognition dawned and his frown deepened.

''She's cut her hand,'' Lucky supplied, knowing he was going to have to explain to Palone a few things later. ''Tell Summ I need disinfectant and a bandage.''

''Right away, sir.''

''Then have a car brought around. We'll be leaving shortly.''

As Palone was ducking back out of the room, his eyes took in the disheveled study.

Lucky said, "We'll get someone to clean this up later."

When they were alone again, Lucky turned back to Elena. She had picked up a picture of Vito and Grace holding a baby. "Where's my brother?"

"Milo's dead."

"Dead?" She bit her lip.

"It happened about six weeks ago."

"How did he die?"

"He was killed."

"By who?"

"A man named Stud Williams."

"Williams? Isn't that the man Rhea was once married to?"

"Yes. Her ex-husband," Lucky clarified. "He's dead, too. He was in a car accident on his way back to prison after his recent breakout." He offered her the story filed at the police department. She didn't need to know that Vito had been responsible for Williams not making it back to prison.

"I don't understand."

"It's complicated."

"I'm sick of hearing that word, Lucky!"

Her voice was full of anger as she stepped forward, her hand raised as if she meant to strike him. But before it could connect, Lucky grabbed her wrist and pulled her up against him. "Take it easy," he soothed.

She tried to wriggle free. "Let me go."

"*Facilmente,* Elena. Easy." He gripped her arms. "We can't change the past."

She pushed away from him, stumbled back, almost losing her balance. "I don't want to change anything. I just want to know why my mother no longer looks like that!" She pointed to the portrait on the wall. "Treat me with the same respect *you* would expect, Lucky. I know you would demand nothing less than the truth, and I won't settle for less, either.''

She was right, he would demand the truth. A small voice inside his head whispered, *Tell her. She deserves to know.*

But could she handle it? All of it?

Frank hadn't thought she could, or he would have told her. Or had Frank's judgment been checkered by his own ghosts from the past?

''I'm twenty-four, Lucky, and everything I thought and believed in is a lie. My whole life has been a lie.''

The desperation in her eyes reminded Lucky of how helpless he'd felt the day he'd learned who and what he was. He'd been only eight years old when Joey had explained to him what it meant to be the son of a mafioso. He was young, but he had understood fully, and at that moment he had desperately wanted to be someone else's son.

''Let me sleep on it, Elena.'' Even as he warned himself not to reveal too much, Lucky knew he was through lying to her. That before he took her back to Santa Palazzo, he would give her what she wanted. ''If I decided to tell you the truth, I'll have your word that you'll go home afterward. Say it.''

''I'll go home after I hear the truth.''

''I have your word?''

''Yes, my word. Is Vito Tandi like you?''

''Like me?''

''Like you and Frank. A mobster?''

''Were you hoping for better, Elena?''

''I don't know what you mean.'' She chewed on her lip as she rubbed her hands on her thighs. Subtle signs that she was nervous and uncertain.

"When Frank told you about his life here in Chicago, you admitted you already knew he wasn't your father. At that point you must have considered the possibilities. Have you been dreaming about a fairy-tale daddy, Elena? An upstanding citizen in the community? A doctor, perhaps? Or maybe a lawyer?"

"So he is like you."

Feeling her judgment, he said, "Sorry to ruin the fairy tale, Elena."

Her chin lifted. "When do I get to meet him?"

Lucky laughed, then sobered. "You don't."

A knock on the door prevented Elena from protesting Lucky's ridiculous last statement. She stood stiff and angry as he turned to admit a slender Asian woman carrying a small first-aid kit, a blue parrot riding her shoulder.

"Benito said there was an accident." When the woman locked eyes with Elena, she gave a gasp of surprise. The noise sent the parrot into flight, flapping his wings to reach his perch.

"Elena," Lucky said, "this is Summ, the housekeeper."

Elena held out her hand as the woman came toward her. "I'm pleased to meet you. I'm—"

"No need to tell me." Summ squeezed Elena's hand. "You are miracle. The one I have been praying for. Wonderful miracle." She raised Elena's hand to examine the cut. "Come, I fix."

Summ's gaze swept the room as she placed the first-aid kit on the coffee table, but she never said anything about the mess, nor did she acknowledge Lucky as he came forward to stand at Elena's side. The minute the wound was cleaned and bandaged, he said, "You can leave now."

The housekeeper stood slowly, almost reluctantly. "When should *shujin* expect visit from *musume?* It is late, but such a miracle will give him great pleasure."

"There will be no visit," Lucky said.

Elena watched the little woman straighten her spine. "No visit? *Shujin* must see *musume*."

"No." Lucky shook his head. "And you will keep what you know to yourself. *Capiche?*"

Summ scowled. "You make mistake. Big mistake." She angled her head in Elena's direction. "Tell him, *musume*. Tell *wakui shujin* to let you see father." To Lucky, she said, "You responsible for giving peace in death or not. Up to you. But if you deny my *shujin* peaceful heart on journey, I pray evil spirit eat your liver."

When Summ headed for the door, Elena followed her. "Wait a minute. What do you mean, in death?"

"Never mind, Elena." Lucky pointed to the door. "Leave us, Summ. You've said enough."

"I don't think she's said near enough," Elena argued. "Stay, please."

"Go." Lucky opened the door, shouted, "Palone!" Benito appeared, ducking his head as he entered the room. "Yes, sir?"

"Escort Summ to her room," Lucky told him. "If she resists, toss her over your shoulder."

The bodyguard glanced at Summ, then back at Lucky. "You want me to touch her?"

Lucky arched a black brow. "If you think you can herd her, be my guest. But do it quickly, Palone."

"*Gwaak!* Big mistake, moron. *Gwaak!*"

Lucky gave the bird a dirty look, while Summ offered Lucky one in kind.

Elena stood back and observed the situation, noting that neither Lucky nor Summ looked as if they were going to back down. On the other hand, Benito Palone looked reluctant but resigned to doing as he was told.

As he advanced, Summ spun around and waved her hand. "You are big fool," she said, then shrieked, "Chansu, attack!"

The minute the words were out of the woman's mouth, Benito Palone spun on his heel and scrambled for the door as Chansu lifted off his perch, sailing out the door after Palone like an eagle hunting a fat rabbit. The guard appeared momentarily confused in the hallway. There was a wild cry from Palone, followed by a victory squawk from Chansu. Then a door slammed and all went quiet.

With a smug look on her face, Summ turned to Lucky. "I bring tea." She eyed the way he was standing. "Sleep better with Matcha so you make wise decision in morning." To Elena she said, "Come, *musume.* I show you to upstairs bedroom."

## Chapter 6

Lucky sat at the breakfast table the following morning listening to Joey's angry voice bounce off the walls like cymbals in an outhouse.

"You knew she wasn't our sister! You've known for weeks!"

Lucky closed his eyes as his brother's roar nearly sent his eyes out the back of his head. He'd been up all night drinking, and he had the absolute worst headache he'd ever had in his life.

When Joey's fist hit the table and a glass flew off it to shatter on the slate floor, Lucky groaned.

As if he was in an interrogation chamber being fired at from both directions, Lucky winced and squinted against the bright beam of light that had found his face through the stained-glass windows.

Joey stood, knocked over the chair.

Again Lucky groaned.

"So Elena is Vito and Grace's daughter, and Frank knew it?" Joey turned and gave Lucky a sour look.

"Yes. I don't think he knew it when he rescued Grace from Vincent's cabin that fateful night, but after they were in Key West and Elena was born, I'm sure he was aware of it. He never put his name on her birth certificate."

Joey shoved his hand's into his pants pockets. "And you're telling me it's because of her eyes?"

"She has Vito's eyes, Joey." Lucky rubbed his temples.

"If you saw that, why didn't I see that?"

"Because you had your mind on Rhea and Niccolo when we where in Florida a week ago. You weren't looking at anything else or anybody." Lucky reached for the second glass of tomato juice that had miraculously stayed upright when the empty one had bounced off the table moments ago. He swallowed a handful of pills, then chased them down with the juice.

"Are you living here now? I thought you didn't intend to move in until after Vito was gone."

"I haven't exactly moved in. Like I said, Palone called last night and told me Vito wanted to see me. Elena was with me. I had no choice but to bring her along."

"You would have had a choice if you had told me the truth weeks ago," Joey argued. "Then she wouldn't be here under Vito's nose."

That was true enough. Lucky leaned back and closed his eyes. This was a mess, and he was responsible for making it worse.

"She knows Vito's her father?"

Lucky nodded. "Yes."

"Where is she now?"

"Upstairs asleep in the orange room."

"What's the orange room?"

"The orange bedroom next to the green bedroom. Down the hall from the blue bedroom."

His brother was looking at him like he'd lost his mind.

Lucky had called Joey an hour ago wanting to catch him before he went to the office at Masado Towers. He'd decided to tell him about Elena and to come clean with how long he'd known the truth. It wasn't going well. Not that he'd expected it would.

"Have you called Frank and told him she's here?" Joey asked.

"Yes. I also told him that Elena knows that Vito's her father. He chewed my ass off on the phone and wants me to fly her home immediately. I told him that wasn't going to happen."

"And why not?"

"Because she's determined to meet Vito."

"Like that's going to happen." Joey snorted. "Hell, just take her back and drop her in Frank's lap and let him deal with her."

"You sound just like Frank. He says if I'm not willing to bring her by force, then he's coming to get her."

"He can't do that! He's dead!"

Lucky winced as the thunderclap of words sent a flash of lightning through the top of his head. "I told him that, Joey. But he's worried, okay? I told him I wouldn't let anything happen to her. And that I'd get her back to Santa Palazzo as soon as possible."

"Did he agree to that?"

"He gave me twenty-four hours. So you're mad at me, too, right?"

"Hell, yes, I'm mad. I thought we were in this to-gether. Then I learn you're keeping secrets."

"True, I kept a few things from you. But at the time you had your hands full with Rhea and Niccolo."

"I'm not buying that." Joey leaned forward and rested his hands on the table to level his brother with a questioning look. "Just like I'm not buying that there isn't more you're not telling me. Why can't you do as Frank asked? Why can't you just toss her in the plane and fly her back and forget her?"

Lucky leaned back in his chair—a green leather commander chair that was driving the pain in his back out his tailbone. "I can't, Joey. Not yet. I will, but only after—"

"I learn the truth."

Her sexy voice sent Lucky and Joey's eyes to the open archway that led into the kitchen. Elena, wearing an orange velvet robe, was leaning against the frame.

"You should still be sleeping," Lucky heard himself say, noting the dark color beneath her eyes.

"While you and—" she eyed Joey "—your brother conspire to get rid of me?"

"There are things you don't understand," Joey said.

"Yes, it's complicated." She eyed Lucky. "You look terrible."

"Thank you. I feel worse than terrible, so I'll take that as a compliment."

"Have you decided when I can see my father?" she asked. "Summ said he sleeps late, so after lunch—"

"It's not going to happen," Joey offered.

Elena's hands went to her hips. "I will see my father before I leave this house. You can count on that, Joey."

"What you can count on, sweetheart, is leaving within the hour."

"Joey." Lucky slowly stood, his head ready to explode. His nagging back pain prevented him from standing straight. "She'll go after I clear up a few of her questions."

His brother stared at him with a look of disbelief. "You're going to let her see him, aren't you?"

Lucky didn't answer.

Joey ran his hands through his short black hair. "Are you crazy? If Vito learns that he's got a daughter, he'll know that Grace never—"

"Joey!"

His brother snapped his mouth shut.

"Died?" said Elena. "That's what you were going to say, right?"

"Elena—"

She came forward. "I told you last night, Lucky, that I'm not as naive as I look. Frank told me Mother was supposed to have died years ago. But before he told me that, I researched her injuries. I know they weren't caused by an accident. I know she was…beaten. Complicated. Oh, yes—" Elena's gaze shifted from Lucky to his brother "—I would agree with you on that, Joey. But that's not going to stop me from meeting my father. Or learning everything I can about the night my mother was nearly beaten to death."

Lucky stepped forward and took her by the arm and steered her back to the kitchen entrance. "Go to your room, Elena," he insisted. "Stay there until I come for you."

"As you wish, *wakai shujin*," she sniffed, then pulled away from him and left.

"What the hell did she call you?" Joey asked.

"It's not important." Lucky headed back to the table, stopping to right the turned-over chair. Pointing to it, he said, "Sit, Joey. We need to talk about something else."

Joey's dark eyes narrowed as he sat on the chair. "Don't tell me there's more bad news."

Lucky sat on the chair across from his older brother. "I ran into Moody Trafano last night."

"Trafano? Where?"

"At the Shedd."

"I thought we agreed you would avoid that place until we were ready to tell the world you're Vito's heir."

"I was there looking over my newly acquired assets."

"You mean you were drinking?"

Lucky shrugged. "That, too."

"So what about Trafano?"

"He made the first move, Joey."

His brother swore. "I don't like the sound of that."

Lucky chewed on the words a minute, then finally spit them out. "I shot him."

"You…shot him." Joey sank back in the chair. "Is he dead?"

"No. I shot him in the knee."

"You shot him in the knee." Joey repeated. "That's just great, Lucky. You know what you've done, don't you?"

"I know."

"Dammit!" Joey stood, the chair falling over again with a crash. He rubbed the back of his neck, unbuttoned his gray suit jacket and started to pace. "Have you talked to Jacky about this?"

"He was there shortly after it happened."

"Vinnie D'Lano has already promised he's going to get me for dumping Sophia," Joey reminded Lucky. "When he hears about this on top of Vito making you his heir, there's going to be all-out war."

"It was bound to happen, anyway, Joey," Lucky reasoned, not liking how that sounded. He wasn't into making matters worse. He was the fixer, after all. "I figure we have about a week or two before D'Lano gets out of jail. Once that happens, he'll hit us. I would have walked away if I could have, Joey. But I was flat on my back. My legs…" Lucky refused to go on. "It was either him or me, with Elena in the middle."

The look Joey offered him said he understood. He walked to the narrow stained-glass windows lining the room to the southeast. "I'll talk to Jacky and find out the status on Moody. See if he can pinpoint how soon Vincent can be released from jail." He turned from the window. "Until you hear from me, you stay here."

"Hiding out? There's no way, Joey."

Joey pointed his finger at his brother. "You listen to me, little brother. I'm not burying you alongside Frank's empty casket. We've come too far to get careless now. You were there for me and Jacky the past two months. If we stick together we're unbeatable. To the end and beyond, it's what we promised. *Capiche?*"

*"Eternamente, fratello,"* Lucky agreed. "Always."

"So it's settled, then. You'll remain here at Dante Armanno until I talk things over with Jacky and see where we stand."

Elena returned to her room to find Summ making her bed. Today the housekeeper was wearing a silk dress in a rich copper brown, her black hair loose and pulled back from her small face by a wide copper clip.

"Good morning," Elena said, noticing a teapot and cups on the small table, along with a plate of pastries.

"Did you sleep well?" Summ rounded the bed to stuff the pillows into two orange velvet pillow shams.

"Yes. A short night, but the bed was soft and warm." She glanced at the long wooden bench at the foot of the bed where a pair of black silk pants and a matching loose shirt lay.

"I did not see any luggage. I thought maybe you might like clean clothes."

Elena had packed light when she'd left Key West. So light, in fact, that she had one small bag at the motel where she was staying, and the clothes inside wouldn't keep a Chicago fly warm. She reached out and sent her fingers over the soft satin. "Thank you, Summ. It's thoughtful of you."

Smiling, the housekeeper moved to the table in front of a two-story window overlooking a courtyard covered in snow. The cold weather outside only served to make Elena more aware of the warmth inside. Whatever had drawn her to the house last night still held her captivated.

*"Musume?"*

Elena looked over her shoulder. "What does that mean?"

"It mean daughter. Sit, *musume,* and I serve you tea." Summ motioned to one of the tufted chairs with elegant wooden legs. "Need strength today."

Elena pulled the orange robe close around her hips and sat. "What's my father like?"

As Summ poured the tea, Elena caught the scent of cinnamon. "Father very smart." Summ shrugged. "Gruff like bear, but kind." She placed the tea on the table in front of Elena, then pointed to the pastry. "Sweet, but not made with sugar. Won't destroy pretty figure. You like."

Elena smiled. "I'm sure I will."

Summ sat, her slender body almost childlike. But she was no child. She was a very wise woman who last night had stood up to the giant named Benito, and to *wakai shujin.*

"What does *wakai shujin* mean?"

"It mean young master," Summ offered. "Has he agreed to let you see your father?"

"I think…maybe."

Summ nodded. "Good. Father need to see *musume*."

"I believe Lucky thinks so, too."

Summ eyed Elena. "He is good man. Also gruff like bear."

Elena pictured Lucky's rebellious black hair and last night's unshaven jaw. "Yes, he is hairy like a bear, too."

They shared a chuckle.

"Want to hear story about hairy bear? It is story about legendary fight in alley when he was only fifteen. *Shujin* say story earn him much respect. Make him feared by many."

Elena reached for one of Summ's sugarless pastries, anxious to hear the story.

"It was nighttime, and in those days he was known as Nine-Lives Lucky. He…"

As Summ told the story of how Lucky had entered an alley in Little Italy to save his brother and friend from a gang of ten, Elena sipped her tea, completely absorbed. It was an unbelievable story. The kind of fiction that would have made a good movie.

Summ ended the story with, "*Shujin* say he is like Armanno, the great warrior in Sicily."

Elena sat silent. Mesmerized. Suddenly she felt Summ's eyes on her and she blinked. "What is it, Summ?"

"You look like your mother's picture on wall, but you have your father's eyes. That is why I stare. Forgive, please." She bowed her head. "It will make losing *shujin* not so hard knowing that he lives in you."

"Losing him? What do you mean?"

Summ glanced up. "You do not know?"

"Know what?"

"Your father is sick, *musume*."

"Sick?"

A long minute lapsed before Summ said, "Father has hungry disease in throat."

"Cancer?"

Summ nodded, tears glistening in her eyes. In that moment Elena knew that she was more than just a housekeeper. She was in love with her father. Did he feel the same way about her?

"How long have you worked for him?" Elena asked.

"Twenty years." She poured Elena another cup of tea. "Your mother is still living?"

Knowing how important it was for everyone to believe Grace was dead, Elena had no trouble lying. "No," she said. "She passed away a few years ago. Do you know the story about my mother's life with my father? About the night she had her…accident?"

"Accident?"

"When she was hurt?" Elena carefully explained.

"Your father never talked about wife. Very painful for *shujin*."

"Because she left him?"

"Because she lie to him." Summ sipped her tea. "Your mother betrayed your father with father's friend. *Wakai shujin's* father."

"And do you know what happened that night?"

"Rumor say the two of them were taken away and punished."

The words sent chills up Elena's spine. "Was my father the one who punished them?"

Summ lowered her head.

"Please," Elena pressed. "Was he the one who punished them?"

"*Shujin* sorry for whatever pain he caused wife. Memories very painful."

Elena stiffened in the chair. "Then he was the one." Her voice broke and she closed her eyes. She hadn't wanted it to be so, but she had feared it was true. He had discovered that his wife was unfaithful to him, and he had beaten her and cut her face in a rage to punish her. And then he had taken Frank's eye.

That had to be why Frank wanted to protect her from the truth. Vito Tandi was the one who had tortured her mother. He was the monster.

*It's complicated,* Frank had said. Lucky and Joey had used the same word. Frank had said, *Your father doesn't know you exist. Can never know.*

Elena shivered in spite of the warm robe. How could she face him now? How could she look her father in the eye knowing he was the one responsible for her mother's life of pain?

It all made sense now. The entire, *complicated,* ugly truth. Elena heard herself say, "Has he suffered? The cancer, I mean. Is it painful?"

"Very painful. Torture him day and night."

Elena nodded, glad to hear it. Vito Tandi deserved to suffer for what he'd done. No, her father deserved to die.


Tired of waiting for Lucky to show up, Elena left her room a few minutes before noon dressed in the black satin pants and shirt Summ had given her. She descended the steps feeling as if she was wearing pajamas, but that was ridiculous. The high-collared shirt had complicated frog hooks that went almost to her throat, and the pants were a perfect fit.

Chilled, she remembered the fireplace in the living room and now sought it out. As she entered the room, she saw the parrot, his feathers a bright blue, balanced on the edge of a high-back chair occupied by a rotund man with a bald head. She was about to back out the door when the bird let out a loud squawk, telling the man that someone was there.

When their eyes met, Elena knew it was him: her father.

She should have turned and fled, and she wanted to. But she couldn't move. It was as if her feet were wooden blocks that had been nailed to the floor.

She watched as he reached for a metal walker that stood beside his chair. Sliding forward, he hefted his weight upward, took a second to gain his balance, then started forward.

Again she wanted to run, but she just stood there while he closed the distance between them. The only noise was the scrape of the walker against the floor.

It was obvious it was a struggle to reach her. But he kept moving closer and closer until the metal walker slid to a halt three feet from where Elena stood trembling. She was finally face-to-face with the man who had carved up her mother's beautiful face. Face-to-face with the man who had beaten Grace until he had split her skull open.

"I hate you," she said. "You're a monster."

"Who hates me?" he demanded. "You, who has my Grace's face, but not her...eyes? Who are you?"

In that moment if she'd had a gun, Elena knew she would have aimed it at her father and pulled the trigger.

"Speak!"

His swollen hands kept a death grip on the metal bars of the walker as he stared her down. Elena stared back, their eyes so similar she almost felt as if she was staring into a mirror. Suddenly she had to say it, had to hurt him, even though it was clear he was suffering from a disease that ravaged him from the inside out. "I've come to look at the monster," she taunted. "To see what kind of animal could do such a thing."

"Do what thing?"

Elena wanted to say more, to do more. She wanted to scream at him and knock him on his ass. Lucky was right. She had wanted a father she could be proud of, not an animal with no conscience.

Her disappointment and anger boiled over, and she said, "Listen, you…you poor excuse for a human being, I'm Grace's daughter. Your daughter."

His eyes widened. "What! Daughter? I have no daughter."

"Well, I'm not Frank's, though I wish I were. So, Daddy," she mocked, "when are you going to die so I can dance on your grave?"

A ruddy red stain rose over Vito's cheeks. A second later, he dropped his head.

"Oh, no, you don't," she said. "Don't you dare look away! Look at me! Look at me, and remember how she looked before you cut her and beat her head in! Look! Look at me, *Daddy*. Look, and remember *your* Grace!"

He answered her challenge and raised his head.

To Elena's horror and surprise, the tears on his florid cheeks were flowing like a river. Then his knees buckled and he crumbled to the floor.

"You knew about her and you were never going to tell me? You knew I had a daughter? An heir? Bastard!"

It had been an hour since Lucky had carried Vito to his room. A long hour of listening to the man rage like a mad bull.

His strength finally sapped, Vito now lay on the bed, his mood black. His tortured throat was no longer able to withstand his shouting.

Lucky said, "You're right. I never intended to tell you. I thought it would be better for her."

"You son of a bitch! How long have you known about her?"

"A month. Maybe a little longer."

"So Grace didn't die at the cabin that night."

"No. I don't have the details—" he did, but he wasn't going to share them "—but Frank got her out of there and to a hospital in time to save her life. Later, when she was well enough to travel, he took her out of state and changed her name."

"And she was pregnant?"

"Yes."

"With my child."

"Do you have a problem believing that?"

Vito looked away.

"I didn't think so," Lucky said softly. "All you have to do is look at her to know the truth of it."

"All these years I've lived believing Grace died that night." He looked up. "What about her? Where is my Grace now?"

"She's dead," Lucky lied, knowing he didn't have a choice. "She died a few years ago. But she lived long enough to raise your daughter."

"Raise her as Frank's daughter, you mean?"

"Yes. Grace never fully recovered from her ordeal. She lost her memory that night and never regained it. There was some brain damage."

Vito closed his eyes. After a long while, he said, "I thought you were an honorable man, Armanno."

"Elena's safety is more important than your opinion of me, old man. If her identity is discovered by one of your enemies, what do you think they would do to her? Vincent D'Lano would like nothing better than to take revenge on you through your daughter."

Vito's face paled. "You can't let that happen."

"No, I can't," Lucky agreed.

"You must protect her."

"I intend to. But that could be difficult. She insists on learning the truth about her mother and you. She wants details."

Vito winced. "She can't know what went on that night at D'Lano's cabin."

"She already knows some of it. Enough to make her determined to get the facts."

Vito shook his head. "Elena must never know the extent of Grace's suffering. Never. You need to send her away. Back to wherever she's been living. Wherever this place is that Frank supplied for them. I underestimated your father. I never suspected he was hiding Grace from me all these years. When he died, it must have pained Elena greatly."

It was critical that Vito continue to think Frank was as dead as Grace. Lucky said, "The news was a shock to her, but she's a strong woman." He turned away, not liking how Vito was looking at him.

"Does my daughter know how you feel about her?"

"How I feel?"

"I am sick, not stupid. And I think we both agree that my daughter is very beautiful."

Lucky faced Vito. "My loyalty to my family, as well

as yours, makes her my responsibility. Nothing more, old man.''

''I think you would prefer it that way. Less complicated, huh?''

Lucky was beginning to hate that word.

''How long will she be staying?''

''D'Lano is still in jail, but once he's out, he's going to come gunning for us,'' Lucky said. ''I don't want Elena anywhere near here when that happens.''

Vito eyed Lucky, and he knew the old man's mind was again churning. ''My daughter's safety weighs heavy on you. This is good. It is true you have a responsibility to both families. Your own and mine. I will rest easier in death, Armanno, knowing this.''

## Chapter 7

"**S**he's locked herself in," Summ told him as Lucky approached her in the upstairs hallway.

He said, "Vito is asking for you. Go to him."

She hesitated as if she was unsure who needed her more. "*Musume* is very upset. I—"

"Don't worry. Elena, I can handle. But Vito—" Lucky smiled "—you have more experience there."

The housekeeper blushed, seeming to like hearing that. "I will be gentle but firm. You will also be gentle with *musume*. Yes?"

Lucky's smile never wavered. "Yes."

She reached out and patted his arm. "You are honorable man. I see this in your eyes the first time we meet. Very proud to serve *wakai shujin*."

After Summ left to see to Vito, Lucky rapped on the door. "Open up, Elena."

"Go away."

"We need to talk."

"Not now!"

Lucky swore in Italian, rapped harder on the door. "I'm not going away."

There was a long minute of silence, then the door opened a crack. Enough to allow him to get his boot inside. "I'm listening. Say what you have to say, then leave me alone."

"Let me in."

"No."

"Dammit, Elena." He shoved open the door, sweeping her off her feet and into his arms at the same time. Still holding her, he slammed the door closed. He was about to give her a piece of his mind when he noticed her red nose and eyes.

She turned away in an attempt to hide her face. "Okay, you're stronger than I am even with a sore back and unreliable legs. Now put me down."

The fight had left her voice, and he slid her down the front of him, but he didn't let go of her. "You look terrible."

"Thank you. I feel worse than terrible," she confessed. "I'll take that as a compliment."

His words from that morning offered back to him made him smile. He raised his hand and sent his fingers into her hair to move it away from her troubled face. "This has been a helluva two days."

"Finally we agree on something."

"You were pretty hard on your father, Elena. I just left him, and—"

"Hard on him?" She shoved at Lucky's chest to get free, and he let him go. "I'm not finished with him yet. Not nearly finished."

"*Facilmente,* Elena."

"Don't you tell me to take it easy!"

"Let me say something."

"Not if you're going to condone what he did."

"Listen to me."

"No!" She held up her hand. "I don't want to hear you sticking up for him. It's obvious that's your intent, and I don't want to hear it. You never had to listen to my mother night after night. He never lived with the moaning. Well, I lived with it. Me! Every night!" She turned away, hugging herself. "Summ told me he's the one. He was the one who took a knife to my mother's face." She turned back and glared at him. "How can you condone that?"

"I don't. But you're wrong." Lucky could see that Elena was out for revenge. She hadn't just come to Chicago for a name and the truth. She'd come on a mission to avenge her mother. Carefully he said, "Vito wasn't the one who hurt your mother, Elena. It's true he was there that night, but he didn't touch Grace. He tried to keep her from being hurt."

"That's not true. Summ told me—"

"What she told you was a rumor. The same rumor I've heard since I was a boy. But it's not the truth. Your father didn't do it, Elena. He never tortured Grace."

"Then who?"

The venom in her voice was thick with need for justice. Lucky decided to give Elena a way out. "Carlo Talupa was the one, Elena. Chicago's boss of bosses."

"Well, there is going to be a need for a new boss," she snapped. "Because I'm going to kill him."

"There is no need for that, Elena. He's already dead."

"He's dead. When? How?"

"A week ago. He was shot."

"By whom?"

Lucky shrugged. "The police aren't sure. He had many enemies."

He watched her physically relax. On a sigh, she conceded, "Then it's all over."

"Over?"

"Yes. I wanted the truth. You said you would give it to me. The truth about how and why. Mother betrayed my father with Frank, and Carlo Talupa punished them. That's the truth, right?"

He had cheated her out of the details, but she looked satisfied. Lucky nodded. "Yes, that's the truth."

"I need to speak to my father," she said suddenly.

"He's resting at the moment. You can speak to him a little later. Tonight, before I fly you home."

"Home? I can't go home now."

Lucky scowled at her. "We had a deal. You wanted a name. You have a name. You wanted to meet your father, and you managed to pull that off, too. You're going home, Elena."

"I didn't go behind your back. I walked into a room and he was there."

"It doesn't make any difference. What's done is done. I've held up my end, and now it's your turn to do the same."

"I made that deal before I knew my father was dying. You didn't tell me he was ill. I can't just meet him, accuse him of being a monster, say I'm sorry, then leave."

"Yes, you can. You will."

"No, I won't."

"It's dangerous for you to be here."

"This place is like a fortress. That's a lame excuse to send me home, Lucky."

"You're leaving."

"I'm not!" She turned away, and Lucky knew she was fighting tears. He reached for her before he thought it through. Spinning her around, he pulled her into his arms. "Dammit, Elena, don't do this."

Instead of fighting him, she pressed her body into his, and buried her face against his chest. "*Piacere,* Lucky. Let me stay."

"You know I can't."

She slid her arms around his waist and clung. "Just for a little while. A day or two. Three at the most."

"No."

She looked up at him, tears heavy in her eyes. "I'll do whatever you say while I'm here. I won't leave the estate. I won't make any trouble. I promise."

It was then that Lucky knew she would get her way. He wasn't going to be able to send her back to Santa Palazzo. Not yet, anyway. A few days, he decided. He had already tightened up security. Vinnie was still in jail.

"Kiss me," she whispered. "I know you want to. And I want you to."

She went up on tiptoe, her hands sliding up his back. Her scent wrapped around him, and he felt her soft breasts against his chest. He locked gazes with her. "This is no good, Elena. A bad idea."

Her lips parted and she brushed them against his, torturing him into taking what he wanted. He covered her mouth and sent his tongue inside quickly, sliding along the roof of her sweet mouth. He heard her moan, and he tugged her closer. Sent his tongue deeper. Exploring. Tasting. Stroking.

She angled her head and opened her mouth wider. Offered him more. Whatever he wanted to take. He knew he should back away. Knew he should at least slow down.

He loosened his hold on her waist and ran his hands over her hips, but instead of pushing her away, he lifted her slightly and pressed his swollen shaft against her.

She was wearing black satin pants, and he could feel all of her, every curve, all of her heat.

He kissed her until his breath ran out, then backed off just enough to let her come up for air. To resupply his own lungs. It was as he lowered his head to kiss her once more that he realized what she was up to. Last night she had been willing to do anything to get her father's name. And today she was again willing to make sacrifices to get what she wanted.

Angry that he had allowed her to con him, he let her go. "I told you once before that I was the wrong man to play games with, Elena."

His brittle words had her stepping back. "What?"

"You heard me."

"You think I'm seducing you to buy more time with my father?"

"That's exactly what I think."

She rubbed his kiss off her mouth with the back of her hand. "Get out."

He strolled to the door. Over his shoulder, he said, "Well, it worked. Copping a feel and getting a taste of you has bought you a week." He turned and faced her. "When you speak to your father, don't mention where you've been living. Oh, and as I expected he would, he asked about Grace. I told him she died a few years ago. Stick to the lie, Elena. Things are already complicated enough.''

It was late afternoon when Elena worked up her courage and went looking for Summ. She found her in the kitchen putting together a supper tray.

By the sadness in Summ's eyes when she glanced up from the tray, it was clear the housekeeper was troubled. Elena said, ''I'm sorry, Summ. To understand why I did what I did, you would have had to have known my mother and witnessed her pain. I'm not excusing my behavior, but when you said it was my father who had tried to kill my mother, I—''

''No, I did not say that. I tell you only what story I hear, not the story I believe. Father, hard man, but good man. Love wife.''

''Is that tray for him?''

''Yes. He is in living room by warm fire.''

''I would like to take the tray to him, if I may.''

Summ nodded. ''I make mistake. Say wrong thing. So sorry.''

''No. I jumped to the wrong conclusion. It wasn't your fault.''

Moments later Elena found her father seated in a leather chair close to the huge stone fireplace. An open book was turned over on his lap and his head was tipped back, his eyes closed.

He must have sensed that someone was there. He blinked opened his eyes, focused on her. ''Your mouth is as beautiful as your mother's. Your tongue twice as sharp.''

Elena slid the tray onto the table next to him. She uncovered a plate of pasta and a breast of chicken. Unwrapped a basket of rolls before sitting down on a leather ottoman a foot away.

After a long awkward minute of silence, she said, ''I came to apologize. I was wrong. Misinformed, you could say. It's no excuse, but I—''

''Turn your face so I can look at you, *figlia*.''

Elena did as he asked, sat quietly while Vito studied her Grace-like features. ''Lucky tells me your mother is no longer alive. That she passed away. I am sorry.''

Elena nodded, played the game, as Lucky called it. ''Yes. She never remembered any of what happened to her.''

''That was for the better,'' he said. ''I suppose that means she never remembered me, either?''

''I'm afraid not. Her injuries were extreme, and she never regained her memory. Not that night, or anything before it.''

''What about her mind? Was she—''

''Her mind was alert. But she lived with physical handicaps.'' Elena leaned forward, took the book titled *The Spirituality of Zen* and set it aside, then placed the tray in his lap. ''Eat while the food is hot. It smells wonderful.''

''Summ is a good cook,'' he acknowledged, then took a bite of pasta. ''Lucky tells me that you just recently learned about me. That since your mother's death, you've been living—'' he looked up from his plate ''—by the ocean.''

Elena didn't agree or disagree. She didn't even blink.

Vito grinned. "It was a guess. Your tanned skin," he explained. "It suggests a sunny climate. Am I right?"

"I enjoy being outside," Elena admitted. "Lucky warned me to stick to only what is relevant. Please don't ask me where I've been living."

"All right." He turned his head and coughed.

"So Lucky Masado is your heir."

"Yes. But had I known about you, it would not have been necessary."

"I don't expect you to change anything. I don't want anything from you. I just wanted to meet my real father."

"And so you have. What do you think of him?"

"I think I would like to get to know him better," Elena confessed.

"I would like to get to know my daughter, too. But there is not much time. Tell me something about yourself. What do you do when you are home?"

"I work part-time at a health clinic. I'm a therapist. When I was young I used to massage Mother's temples and try to make her pain go away. Sometimes it helped, and that's how I became interested in myofascial release."

"Which is?"

"It's a hands-on approach to treating physical trauma through massage."

"And it can relieve pain?"

"Yes."

"You will have to show me."

Elena felt herself relax. "Maybe we could get a massage table sent to the house. If there's room, I mean."

"There is plenty of room, *figlia.*"

"All right. Lucky tells me I have a week to spend with you."

"A week?"

Elena wasn't going to discuss what had bought her more time. Lucky believed she'd manipulated him, and that had been her intention. That is, until she'd fallen under the spell of his lips and hands.

"Yes, a week. Unless, of course, you can change his mind and get him to give me two."

"Change Lucky Masado's mind? I don't think that's possible. He is a man who rarely changes his mind about anything."

Softly Elena said, "I know you weren't the one who hurt my mother. That the man responsible is dead."

"Yes, Carlo is dead. That is true. But that doesn't excuse my part in your mother's tragedy. I was there when it happened."

"To watch?"

He paused. "No, I believe I went to kill her that night. I was very angry. But when I saw her, I knew I couldn't do it. Even knowing that she had betrayed me with my best friend, I could never hurt my Grace."

Elena watched him closely as she asked the next question. "You loved her even then?"

"Yes, *figlia.* I thought she loved me, too. But time changes things. Feelings. Needs. Frank was around a lot after his wife died. I was busy. Grace was very beautiful." He smiled. "Like you, she was a pleasure to look at. There is no question you are her daughter. My daughter." He sobered. "It was no one's fault that she and Frank…that they fell in love. I say this today, having had years to ponder the situation. But back then, when I learned what was going on, I was furious. A man in disgrace. I became a mafioso out for blood.''

"You hurt Frank."

"Yes. Frank understood why I had to do it."

"Even after you took his eye?"

"Better his eye than his life, huh?"

"If he had died that night, Mother would have, too. And I would never have been born."

"All day I have thought of this. I am grateful to Frank for taking Grace away to someplace safe. Grateful he raised my daughter for me. We will send out for one of these massage tables, huh? Then you will show me how you helped my Grace. We will have it brought today."

He was having trouble cutting the chicken. "Here, let me, Papa." Elena reached out, took the silverware from Vito's hands and began to slice the chicken into bite-size pieces.

## Chapter 8

Elena pulled the soiled sheets from the massage table and stuffed them into the laundry hamper. The same day she had made peace with her father, he had asked her to make a list of the things she needed to set up a therapy room in the house. By evening the equipment had arrived and within an hour the room across the hall from the study had been transformed into a state-of-the-art massage-therapy room.

What Elena learned in the next three days was that as gruff as her father sounded and as dangerous as his reputation claimed him to be, Vito Tandi was a good man, as Summ had said.

A man who'd survived an emotional tragedy that still haunted him.

Because they both knew their time together was short, they'd spent nearly every waking hour in each other's company. If Elena and Vito weren't in the therapy room working to relieve a degree of his pain, they were seated next to the fireplace, talking. And when Vito's voice gave out, Elena would read poetry to him. He was a great fan of Robert Service.

"*Shujin*'s spirits are high." Summ's voice revealed her delight. "Massage and tea, make him sleep all night. "It is all because of you, *musume*. You are miracle."

Elena spread a clean sheet over the table, then draped a second sheet on top. "He's still in pain. I've been able to reduce the intensity, but I can't make it disappear."

"He wears a smile for the first time in years. Very important medicine."

"We're a good team," Elena acknowledged, giving Summ her share of the credit. The housekeeper was as dedicated to her father as a wife. Maybe more.

Summ blushed. "Yes, we are good team." She patted the therapy table. "How do we get *wakai shujin* on table? He not smile much. Very bad pain in back."

"I know he's in pain. But he's not interested in what I can do to help him."

"Maybe we trick him," Summ suggested.

"Trick him? I don't think so. I don't think that's possible."

Elena hadn't spoken a dozen words to Lucky since he'd kissed her in her bedroom three days ago. He was avoiding her. Even his meals had been eaten in the study. She knew that because she'd seen Summ taking them to him.

"I think on it." The housekeeper tossed her braid off her shoulder. "He need miracle, too."

Elena was still pondering Summ's intentions hours later when she arrived—via Summ's insistence—at the therapy room and came face-to-face with Benito Palone, looking extremely uncomfortable.

"Benito, I thought I was meeting Summ here."

Awkwardly he rubbed his hip. "Summ says you can make the pain in my hip go away. I told her it's not important, but she insisted that you can ease it."

"It's likely," Elena agreed.

He glanced around the room, his dark eyes darting to the table several times.

Elena had no idea why Summ had sent Benito to her, but it didn't really matter. She was willing to do what she could for him. "I'll step outside. Undress and crawl under the sheet. It's your left hip?"

"Yes."

"Lie on your back. I'll return in a few minutes."

Lucky emptied one bottle of Scotch and immediately started on another. All day he'd been seated behind Vito's desk making phone calls, while his back grew stiffer and the pain in his back and hips grew more intense.

He'd been in a great deal of pain from the moment he'd climbed out of bed, and it had only grown worse as the day progressed.

Tandi Inc. was a complex conglomerate, and from the beginning Lucky had known it would require a major commitment. Daily he was putting in the time, but never far from his thoughts was the current situation surrounding Elena.

*Elena.* Lucky's mind returned to the kiss they'd shared in her bedroom. Just going there in his mind sent a rush of heat straight to his groin. He was still damn angry with her for conning him into that kiss. He should have expected she would pull something like that. He'd already seen the lengths she was prepared to go to that first night at the Shedd.

A virgin with a fetish for knives into hardcore manipulation. His mind had been playing with that scenario for days.

Aching inside and out, Lucky carried the bottle to the window and stood staring at the pine trees weighted down with snow. He'd chugged half the bottle by the time the phone rang. It was his cell phone, and he pulled it from his pocket and flipped it open. Recognizing the number, he answered with, "You're late, Frank."

"I lost track of time. I was working with Grace on her therapy. The time got away from me."

"How's that going?"

"I'm getting the hang of it. Grace is improving. The doctors are pleased. I'm pleased, too. How's Elena?"

"Trying to squeeze a lifetime into a week," Lucky admitted.

"Meaning, they're getting along?"

"Yes."

"Will he last the week?"

"I don't know. He's slipping. I can see it. Elena does, too, I'm sure. Still, when he goes, he'll die a happy man. I rarely see him when he's not smiling."

There was silence on the line, then Frank said, "I never believed this could work out. You've managed to pull it off, and I'm grateful, Lucky. I should have faced this sooner. I was a coward and—"

"Don't go there, Frank. You did what you thought was right."

"When you told me you were going to let her stay a full week with Vito, I thought you were crazy. But everything has worked out. I owe you for that, son. How does Elena seem?"

Lucky wasn't sure how to answer that. He'd been keeping an eye on her from a distance. "She's determined to make Vito's last days happy. That's about all

I can tell you.'' He checked his watch. "Time's up, Frank. I'll call you if anything changes.''

He returned the phone to his pocket just as a knock sounded at the door.

"Come in.''

"Time for your tea.''

Lucky watched Summ carry in her bamboo tray with a pot of tea on it. Before she set it down, he said, "I don't feel like tea tonight. Take it back to the kitchen.''

"Need Matcha.'' She motioned to the bottle in his hand. "Drink too much poison. Smell like drunk.''

He glared at her and she headed for the door, but before she left, he said, "Is Elena with Vito?''

"No, he's sleeping. *Musume* with…''

"With who?''

"She's across the hall with Benito.''

Lucky scowled. "What the hell is she doing in there with Palone?''

"He has pain.'' Summ touched her thigh. "Here. Drink Matcha, *wakai*. Good for pain.''

"Then maybe you should brew Palone a pot,'' Lucky grumbled, then tipped the Scotch bottle to his lips.

Summ glared at the bottle. Sniffed loudly, then left.

*You smell like drunk. She's across the hall with Benito. He has pain. Here.*

Lucky unbuttoned his shirt, then pulled it from his jeans, kneading his back with one hand as he emptied the bottle with the other. He paced and drank. Opened bottle number three. Drank, and paced some more.

By the time he left the study a half hour later, he felt no better. In fact, he was feeling worse. He walked across the hall, and without knocking, swung the door open. His sudden unannounced entrance had Elena gasping in surprise, and Palone damn near jumping off the table.

Lucky eyed the situation. Palone's naked chest. His bare feet—size eighteen at least—hanging a good ten inches off the end of the table. He angled his head and stared at Elena. Noticed her flushed cheeks.

She said, "What's wrong? Is it my father?"

"No. Nothing's wrong with him. Something's wrong with me." He leveled Palone a look. "I have a pain."

"That's not really anything new," Elena said, ignoring his sarcasm.

His eyes locked with hers once more. Stared her down.

Her chin went up. "I'm almost finished here. If you want to come back in an hour, I can—"

His eyes never left Elena as he said, "Get out of here, Palone."

"He can't get up," Elena objected. "He's..." She hesitated.

"He's what?"

"He doesn't have any clothes on."

Lucky's nostrils flared. His eyes still on Elena, he said, "You have ten seconds, Palone, to get your ass off that table and disappear."

It took less than five for Benito Palone to grab the white sheet, wrap it around his middle and head for the door. Lucky opened it and Palone ducked his head and left with the sheet outlining his ass.

The sight fueled Lucky's anger, and he slammed the door hard behind the guard. When he turned around, Elena had moved back to the table and was stripping off the bottom sheet. He watched her for a moment as she rolled it into a ball and tossed it in a hamper.

Her back was to him, and he studied her narrow hips

and long legs. She was wearing the same black outfit she'd worn that day in her bedroom. Those damn shiny pants and that slippery shirt that outlined her nipples and reminded him that he knew firsthand what she looked like underneath. That sheer blue bra he'd uncovered days ago had been permanently branded into his memory.

He waited for her to turn so he could see if her nipples were visible. Waited, then said, "So what's wrong with Palone?"

She spun around, nipples perky as hell. "He has an old injury that gives him pain in his thigh in the wintertime. I think arthritis has set into his sacrum."

"His what?"

"The coccyx region."

Lucky shifted his eyes from her chest to her face, tried to block out the vision of Elena touching Palone's...coccyx region.

She started to spread a clean white sheet over the one already in place. He watched her hands slide over the smooth cotton, envisioned them moving over flesh. Palone's flesh.

"It's late, Lucky, and as I've already said, your pain is nothing new. So what is this all about?"

"Palone gets paid to be on his feet, Elena, not lying on his back."

Her hands stilled on the sheet. She looked up. "What does that mean?"

He didn't know what it meant. Yes, he did. He didn't want her touching Palone. "In Key West you worked at this sort of thing?" He motioned to the table. "This was your job, touching men?"

"Touching men? Mostly I concentrated on my mother's therapy. But it's true, when I'm home I work a few days a week at a health center. And yes, some of my patients are men.'' She tucked the corners of the sheet.

''Did you like touching Palone?''

She looked up again, her attention shifting to the bottle in his hand. ''You're drunk, Lucky. Go sleep it off.''

''I don't get drunk anymore.''

She started for the door, but before she reached it, he blocked her exit. She backed up, rounded the table. ''What's wrong with you? Why are you acting like this?''

He followed her and set the bottle down on the table between them. Slowly, he pulled off his shirt and tossed it in the direction of a lone chair in the corner. ''I'm here to be touched.'' He reached for the bottle once more, but she grabbed it away from him.

''You've had enough to drink. Too much.'' She set the bottle on a high counter behind her.

''I'm in pain, Elena. Isn't that the magic word for you to go to work?''

She stood there, not saying anything. Just looking at him with her chin high. He reached across the table and gabbed her wrist. ''Come on, Elena. I thought you wanted to touch me. That's what you said a few days ago. You said you wanted my mouth on yours.''

She twisted her arm to shake him off, but the effort failed. He hung on as he rounded the table, grabbed her other wrist and pulled her closer.

''Stop it, Lucky. Let go.''

He forced her hands to his chest, over his nipples. Closed his eyes. ''Touch me, Elena.''

Suddenly she stopped fighting him, and he opened his eyes to find her staring at his mouth. He leaned down to kiss her, but she turned her head away. Softly she said, "Okay, if you want me to touch you, get on my table."

"You know that's not the kind of touching I'm talking about."

She looked up at him. "Maybe not, but it's what you need."

"What I need is to get you out of my head. But that's not going to happen until you're gone." He released her hands and slid his own over her hips, pulling her against his lower body. Slowly he lowered his head, and this time she let him brush his lips over hers. He whispered, "I want on *you,* not this damn table, Elena."

Her hands were still on his chest, the heat from her touch warning him that he'd started something he didn't want to stop. Something he needed to stop.

He kissed her again, then backed off, realizing suddenly that she was right. He must be drunk. He had to get out of there. He turned to retrieve his shirt, letting her get a good look at his scarred back without thinking.

"You're a *vigliacco.*"

He turned around. "What did you say?"

"You heard me. You're a coward."

"Be careful, Elena."

"I'm not afraid of you. But I think you're afraid of me."

Shirt in hand, he laughed. "Afraid of you? I don't think so."

"Prove it."

"And how would I do that?"

"Get on my table."

"As you said, it's late, Elena."

She walked past him, headed for the door. "Take off everything and climb beneath the sheet, Lucky.

Facedown. You can either be on the table when I get back, or gone. It's your choice.''

The scar was like nothing she had ever seen before, Elena thought as she paced the study. Her mother had extensive scars, but this was the longest Elena had ever seen. And she hadn't even seen it in its entirety.

She wanted to find him on the table when she returned, but she wasn't expecting it. She glanced at her watch. Two more minutes. She'd go back in two minutes, and if he was gone…

Her thoughts returned to the scar, anxious to touch it. From the look of it, the knife wound had been extremely deep, the granulation tissue creating secondary adhesions. The lesion guaranteed radical nerve damage. Before she did anything—touched him—maybe she should talk to his doctor.

More than five minutes had gone by, and still Elena wasn't sure she was ready to go back to the therapy room and find Lucky gone.

But what if he wasn't gone?

What if he was naked beneath the sheet?

She touched her lips, unable to deny how much she liked his mouth on hers. She unfastened the clip that held her hair off her neck and reworked the loose pieces back into the twist on the top of her head. Deciding that she'd stalled long enough, she opened the study door and walked across the hall and into the room.

The sight of him on the table brought her up short. As she'd instructed, he appeared to be naked. Her gaze drifted over him. He was lying facedown, the sheet covering his lower body and exposing the enormous scar that followed his spine.

The music she worked to was a meditation CD used

to help relax patients. She walked to where the trim silver stereo sat next to her oils and emollients and hit the button to restart the CD. The low haunting sounds suddenly ate up the silence.

Elena's heart was pounding, and she was afraid he could hear it. She took a deep breath, said, "Are you cold?"

"No."

His voice was low, his face positioned in the doughnut-shaped pillow that allowed him to breathe comfortably.

"First I'm going to palpate the scar," she said, gently folding the sheet down to rest low on his smooth hips. "What I'll be looking for are the most tender points along the spine. Hot spots, I call them."

The sight of Lucky's broad back leading into his narrow waist made Elena's stomach do a nervous flip. She struggled to keep her voice normal. "Those will be the areas I'll want to work on first."

She ran her hand along the scar pressing gently as she followed the vertebrae along his spine. "Here?" she asked. "Is there more pain here?"

"Yes."

"And here?"

"Not so much. But, yes."

She moved lower, pushed the sheet to the rise of his beautiful backside. "And here?"

"Yes."

"I'm going to have you roll onto your back so I can see the path the scar travels and continue to palpate."

He did as she asked and as he started to roll over, she rescued the sheet to keep his gender hidden from her eyes. When he was facing her, she slowly moved the sheet downward, looking for the end of the scar.

The knife that had traumatized him had cut across his hip to his navel. From there it headed downward. Elena's hands stilled, knowing he was watching her. Knowing that if she lowered the sheet farther, she chanced revealing more than just his scar.

"Ten inches. Think you can handle that?"

Elena jerked her head up. "What?"

"The scar." He grabbed her hand. Pressed her fingers into the scar just below his navel. "From here to the end of the scar is ten inches," he clarified. Then he released her hand, grabbed the sheet and flipped it off his right leg.

For a moment Elena was sure he was going to expose himself. It never happened. His big hand gripped the sheet close to his private area to keep it covered, revealing only his leg and the scar that had ripped his stomach at an exaggerated angle to end up on his muscular thigh.

If he was trying to shock her, she wasn't going to allow it. He had a magnificent body, and as much as she enjoyed looking at it, she successfully kept her hands steady as she began to palpate the scar.

There was a tender spot as Elena pressed her fingers into the scar two inches from his navel. "All right," she said, pulling the sheet back over him, "you can roll onto your stomach again."

She guided the sheet once more as he rolled, his hands dropping to rest on the padded rail beneath the headrest.

Now that she knew where the restrictions were based, she knew what would benefit him the most. Touching his right shoulder, she said, "I want you to relax completely. Give your body to me." When he didn't answer, she said, "We'll need a control word between us. A word you can use when you want me to stop if the treatment becomes too painful. It's beneficial, however, to sometimes feel a degree of pain with myofascial release.''

''What's wrong with the word *ouch?*''

Elena smiled. ''Okay. If you like that word.''

She stood at his right shoulder, his head close to her thigh. Afraid he would decide he'd had enough before she could get started, she moved her hands to the first hot spot between his shoulder blades and began to apply pressure to the area.

With scar release the movements were slow, and the pressure needed to remain constant. There was no directing or forcing deep within the layers of fascia, and sometimes there was no moving at all, just waiting—sometimes three to five minutes—before the barrier let go.

Prepared to stay up all night if need be, Elena soon became lost in her work and the feel of Lucky beneath her hands. As the minutes ticked by and each release came, she said a silent prayer, then followed it through, keeping the pressure constant until she felt Lucky's body surrender to her with a deep sigh.

''That's it,'' she whispered. ''Noises are good, too. A moan. I'll even accept swearing.''

She moved to the next tender point. Began the process again. It was slow and laborious work, but she kept at it. Each time she felt the fascia layers move, she knew she was making a difference—relieving a degree of his pain.

Forty minutes later, on a hot spot near the base of Lucky's spine, he expelled a deep guttural groan that made Elena feel victorious. She hated the idea of hurting him, but she knew after the initial pain, he would feel better.

"That time I felt heat," she said softly. "It's called therapeutic pulse, and it means we're making progress."

She stepped away from him for a moment, then returned with an emollient. She poured some into her palm, rubbed her hands together and began to massage his back, then his shoulders. It was important to keep his muscles relaxed.

Before long she tucked the sheet at his waist, exposed his right leg and began to knead the muscles in his thigh, then his calf. She even spent a few minutes on his feet. She took her time, moving on to his left leg to repeat her treatment.

She asked him to roll over once more. Repeated the process.

She lost track of time, caught up in touching him in ways and in places she had only dreamed of touching him. It was after midnight when she finally looked at the clock.

"Now it's very late," she said. "That's all for today." She turned away, put the cover on her jar of massage cream, and when she turned back, Lucky was sitting up, dragging the sheet with him as he stood.

His eyes were heavy-lidded, his movements delayed. The combination of liquor and massage had worked like a sedative, Elena suspected.

He stared at her without saying a word, and she wondered what he was thinking. What he was feeling.

"I hope I didn't hurt you too badly. I never heard the word *ouch*."

He shrugged, continued to stare, his chest rising and falling slowly.

"I should let you get dressed." She headed for the door.

"Elena."

She stopped, turned. "Yes."

"Tomorrow. We do it again?"

"Yes, if you'd like. We could meet while my father is taking his afternoon nap. *Buona notte,* Lucky."

"Good night, Elena."

# Chapter 9

Three days later Vito Tandi passed away quietly in the middle of the afternoon with Grace's name on his lips, Elena at his side and Summ standing vigil over the candles that had continued to burn since that morning, when he hadn't been able to get out of bed.

The candles, Summ claimed, would light Vito's path on his journey into the next life.

It had snowed heavily that day and remained overcast ever since. Yesterday Lucky had arranged a private memorial service as mandated in Vito's will. It had been closed to the public; his staff at Dante Armanno and Lucky and Elena were the only ones in attendance.

The rest of the day Elena had spent with Summ going through old photo albums of her parents during happier times. She had taken Vito's death hard, as Lucky knew she would, but as he'd told Frank, Elena was determined to do the right thing.

She had known her time with her father was short,

and she'd crammed a lot of living into six days. No, it hadn't been enough, but if it was possible to grow to love someone in a week's time, Lucky believed Vito and Elena had truly become father and daughter.

They'd eaten every meal together, and more than once he'd heard laughter coming from the living room— Vito's husky chuckles and Elena's sexy sweet peals of joy.

It was true that Vito's last days on earth had been spent smiling, and Elena was responsible for that. Summ had called her Vito's miracle. And Elena was certainly that.

Secretly she had become *his* miracle, too. In four days his back pain had diminished by half.

"He's been cremated, Miss Tandi," Henry Kendler said. "That was your father's wish, and also that his ashes be given to his housekeeper, Summ Takou. I trust you don't have any objections?"

"No objections," she said softly.

Lucky watched Elena as she offered a sober smile to the lawyer, who sat behind his desk in his office high above the city. They had been listening to the reading of Vito's will for close to an hour.

She bent her head and touched her nose with a damp, rumpled tissue that she'd pulled from her pocket.

"Miss Tandi, are you all right?"

"She's fine," Lucky growled. "Finish up, Kendler, so we can get the hell out of here. It's probably the smell of this place that's making her eyes water. Haven't you ever heard of central air?"

Kendler sniffed the stale air as if he was unsure what Lucky was talking about, then lowered his gaze to the paper on his desk. "I just have a couple more things."

"Well, get on with it."

"Vito wrote you a letter, Mr. Masado." Henry Kendler looked suddenly nervous as his blue eyes, rimmed in shiny wire glasses, darted from Lucky to Elena, then back to Lucky. "Should I read it, sir?"

When Lucky didn't answer, Elena said, "Yes, please."

"No," Lucky held out his hand. "I'll take it."

Once Henry Kendler had handed Lucky the envelope, he ripped it open and silently read.

I'm finally dead if you're reading this, Armanno. Do not forget what you promised me days ago. Should I die before my enemy has been dealt with, we agreed that my burden would become your burden, my responsibilities, your responsibilities. See that Vincent D'Lano dies a painful death and while he is dying remind him why. Tell him Vito sends his best.

About *mia figlia.* This past week has been worth everything I have suffered. Thank you. Elena is all that is left of my Grace. Do what you must to keep her safe. Whatever you must. I understand about the secret trust fund now. I understand more than that, and you have my blessing. Grazie, Armanno. Live well. Love well.

Lucky folded the letter and slid it into the envelope, then into the pocket on his leather jacket.

"Is there one for me?"

Lucky glanced over to see Elena hopeful, if not anxious.

"I'm sorry, Miss Tandi, there is no letter for you. But he did want me to give you this." Kendler produced a large manila envelope and handed it to her.

Elena opened the envelope and looked inside, then pulled out a book and a red velvet box. Inside the box was a ring and necklace.

"They were your mother's," Kendler offered. "Rubies, I believe."

The necklace was one large red ruby in the shape of a teardrop hanging from a gold chain. The ring appeared to be Grace's wedding band—a large ruby surrounded by diamonds. Lucky recognized the poetry book as the same one from which he'd seen Elena reading to Vito. Inside he had inscribed, *To my daughter, Elena Donata Tandi. My Grace in beauty and in spirit. Your loving father, Vito.*

Without any words, Elena closed the book and slipped the ruby necklace around her neck, then slid the ring on the third finger of her right hand.

They left Henry Kendler's office around noon. In Lucky's red Ferrari, he asked, "Are you all right?"

"Yes."

She was avoiding his eyes. Lucky reached out and, gripping her chin, forced her to look at him. "Why does that yes sound like there's something more you want to say?"

She pulled away and wrapped her coat tightly around her—a long black wool coat that Summ and Palone had bought for her days ago, along with a number of other necessities she'd listed for them. "What was in the letter?"

"It was just business."

"Business?" She shook her head. "I don't think so."

"It was," he insisted.

"Listen, you, I can tell when you're lying. If I can't trust you, who can I trust?"

Lucky let the insult roll off his back and turned on

the ignition. His hand on the stick shift, he asked, "Are you hungry?"

"I thought it was too dangerous for me to be away from Dante Armanno. That's why you refused to let me do my own shopping, remember? Why I'm wearing a coat that must weigh fifty pounds."

The coat did look a bit extreme for November. "Are you hungry?" he asked again.

"You're actually asking me out to lunch?"

"You leave tomorrow, Elena. You'll be safe with me in a restaurant this one time. I promise."

"Because I'm with Nine-Lives Lucky, the most feared *soldato* in the city?"

He scowled at her, suddenly realizing that not all her conversations with Vito over the past week had been about family. "If you have no appetite, then you can watch me eat," he told her. "I'm hungry."

"For food that requires a fork and teeth, or just a glass?"

She was trying to pick a fight. Lucky wasn't going to take the bait. He hadn't had a drink in two days and his appetite was coming back. He said, "I'm hungry for some good monkfish."

"And where do you get good monkfish?"

He smiled mainly because she wasn't smiling, then pulled the car away from the curb. "My old neighborhood, where else?"

Caponelli's was a quaint restaurant in the heart of Little Italy. Lucky led Elena through the door fifteen minutes after leaving the parking lot near Henry Kendler's law office.

The cozy restaurant was busy. More than half the tables were taken, and people were waiting to be seated.

While she and Lucky waited, Elena glanced at the pictures on the wall behind the cash register. The one that caught her eye was of three small boys on a green couch. They looked like pure trouble as they grinned into the camera. The middle black-haired boy—maybe three years old—sat balanced on the knees of the other two dark-haired boys. The caption under the picture read: *To the end and beyond. Friends forever. Eternamente. Per sempre.*

When it came their turn to be seated, a gray-haired woman in her early sixties hurried toward Lucky with open arms and a wide smile. "It's about time you showed up. You haven't been here in weeks," Lavina Ward scolded.

Elena didn't expect Lucky's wide smile or the carefree way he scooped up the woman and kissed her on both cheeks. When he set her back on her feet, he said, "Is my usual table open?"

She glanced to a far corner of the room. "You're in luck. Here, let me take your coats and put them in the back."

After Lavina ushered them to the quiet corner spot, she disappeared with their coats. Lucky pulled out a chair for Elena, and once she was seated, he took the chair opposite that allowed him to sit with his back to the wall and gave him a view of the entire room, the entrance and the hallway that advertised rest rooms.

When Lavina returned, Lucky said, "Vina, this is Elena. Elena, this is Jacky's mama."

The woman's smile was genuine when she locked eyes with Elena. "Jackson said you looked like your mother. He just never mentioned how much." She leaned closer, lowered her voice. "My condolences on the passing of your father."

"Thank you," Elena said. "I'm pleased to meet you, Mrs. Ward. You have a charming restaurant."

"I'll bring menus and a bottle of *vino della casa.*" Her eyes shifted to Lucky. "Or do you want—"

"Wine is fine. But we'll forgo the menus. Elena wants to try your famous monkfish and linguine, Vina."

Elena opened her mouth to protest, then just as quickly smiled. "Yes, please. I've heard it's the best in the city."

"I make it with *aglio* and a pinch of *zenzero.* You will like it."

After Lavina returned to the kitchen, Elena refocused on Lucky and found him staring at the ruby cradled in her cleavage.

She'd chosen a black scooped-neck sweater and black pants to wear to the lawyer's office. She touched the ruby. "It's beautiful," she said.

His eyes lingered a moment longer, lingered until Elena felt a warm flush surface on her cheeks. Finally he said, "*Sì,* very beautiful."

Lucky was right about the monkfish. Elena had never tasted anything so delicious. It was understandable why the small restaurant was so popular.

There wasn't one patron in the restaurant, however, whom Lucky didn't take apart from head to toe. Elena noticed he'd taken a special interest in a dark-haired man across the room from them. He was a big man with a face like a bulldog and a scar that disfigured his nose.

"Who is that?" she asked.

"No one you will ever meet. Ignore him." Lucky shoved his empty plate to the side and reached for his wine glass.

He'd had only one glass of wine with his meal, though Lavina had left a full bottle. Elena wondered about that.

Wondered if the therapy sessions had relieved enough pain to negate his need for alcohol, or if something else had caused him to let go of the Scotch. But she knew something was different—he no longer smelled like a distillery.

He emptied his glass of wine as she took the last bite of her fish. When he set the glass down, he asked, "Are you ready?"

"Are we in a hurry?"

"No."

"I liked the fish," she said softly.

"I knew you would. Let's go."

"I thought we weren't in a hurry." She glanced at the table where the man with the ugly nose had been sitting. He was gone.

"I should get you back."

"Before we return to Dante Armanno, would you take me by the house where you and Joey grew up with Frank?" When he looked as though he was going to say no, Elena reached out and took his hand. "Don't say no, Lucky. Please."


It was like many of the neighborhoods in Little Italy, run-down and in need of serious repair. The Masado house was a small two-story brick structure, but a step above the ones on either side. A large oak tree graced the front yard.

Elena climbed out of the Ferrari, noticing the young boy shoveling the snow off the path to Lucky's house. Or trying to. Five boys of similar size were giving him a hard time.

"Stay here," Lucky told her as he rounded the car and strolled up the path. He said nothing as a warning, simply walked into the group of boys and put his arm

around the one with the shovel. Elena heard Lucky call
the boy Tito. She remembered that was the name of the
cab driver's son from the other night.

Suddenly Lucky was holding the shovel, and he had
persuaded four of the boys to back off. Then she heard
him say, "If he stays on his feet, another of you will
take a turn at him. Then another and another. No
knives." Then he smiled at the boys, who were suddenly
fidgeting and eyeing one another with worried looks on
their faces.

One of the boys said, "It's him, ain't it? Nine-Lives
Lucky."

Another nodded. "We're all dead."

"No," Lucky told the boy. "A little smarter tomorrow, maybe. Sore in a few places, but not dead."

It took fifteen minutes for Tito to show the bullies he
knew how to fight. And yes, the boys would be sore
tomorrow, all five of them.

As they walked down the street, each one of them
nursing a bruise or wiping blood, Lucky said to Tito,
"You wait too long to throw your left, *amico.* Twist
your body and use your legs, too. One, two, three, jab.
One, two, three, kick. Mix it up. Move. Always move."
He took hold of the teenager's chin and eyed the growing bruise on his cheek. "Go home. You can finish this
tomorrow. Have you been keeping Lavina Ward's walkway shoveled, too?"

"Yes. Just like you said I should. And her roof."

"Good. Keep up the good work."

Once the boy left, Elena came forward. In the past
week she had gotten to know who Lucky Masado really
was. She knew he was the most feared *soldato* in the
city, but also the most respected. Her father was right.
He was the American Armanno.

"So this is how you used to spend your days as a young boy. Fighting in the street."

He smiled that half smile that told her his body was never without pain. "Sometimes." He gestured to the house. "This is it. Where Joey and I grew up."

"Can we go inside?"

He studied her a moment. "I suppose this is what I get for making you eat monkfish. A tour of my humble beginnings. Though I did notice you almost licked the plate."

His teasing was followed by an awkward moment of silence. Abruptly he took her arm and escorted her up the path. They climbed four steps, then he unlocked the door with a key he'd produced from his jeans. As soon as he closed the door behind them, Lucky said, "I'll turn up the heat."

When he disappeared down the hall, Elena walked into the living room. She noticed a row of pictures on an old upright piano and walked past the couch to look at them. One, she assumed, was a picture of Lucky's mother. She was pregnant, and a small boy stood beside her. She was a pretty woman with dark hair and eyes. She looked happy.

When Elena turned from examining the pictures, she found Lucky standing next to a table a few feet away. She hadn't even heard him enter the room.

He reached out and turned on the lamp. "Seen enough?"

"Have you always lived here?"

"Yes."

"Your mother... Frank said she died."

"Yes. She died in the hospital having me."

It was the first that Elena had heard of that. He held out his hand and she stepped forward and took it. He led her down the hall, then into the kitchen. This room was brighter, the shade at the windows covering only half the glass. He pulled it up, then pointed to the fence that lined the backyard. "See that tree a couple of houses over? The big one with the crazy branch?" He pulled her in front of him. "See it?"

"The twisted branch?"

"*Sì*, that's the one. I fell out of that tree and almost broke my neck when I was four. Got my first scar that day. That white house there." He pointed. "That's where Jacky grew up. Where we all grew up, you might say. I spent more time there the first fifteen years of my life than I did here."

Elena turned, knowing it would put her in his arms. For days she had been able to touch him at will in the therapy room, and it had only served to make her more mesmerized by him. "And this first scar," she said softly, "where is it?"

"Left shoulder."

Elena nodded, remembering it. "Two inches long. More than a scratch."

He stared down at her. "We should go."

"I haven't seen the rest of the house yet."

"It's nothing special, you can see that."

It was special because he'd lived here, but Elena kept her thoughts to herself. He stepped back and they left the kitchen. When she saw the stairway leading to the second level, she headed for it.

"Elena, there's nothing up there. Just bedrooms and a bathroom."

"I'd like to use the bathroom if you don't mind." She turned on the third stair. "Is that all right?"

"First door on the left."

She climbed the stairs, found the bathroom. As she

returned to the hallway minutes later, she left her coat on the stair railing and went room to room in search of Lucky's bedroom. It was the smallest room, the one with the least amount of books and clutter. How she knew that, she couldn't say.

Spying a hinged wooden box on the dresser, she rounded the double bed and opened it. Inside she found several colorful small rocks, a pocket knife and two crudely carved wooden animals.

"This is the second door on the right, Elena."

She jumped. Turned.

Lucky was leaning against the wall. He'd shed his jacket, leaving him in one of his collarless hemp shirts. She liked his shirts, liked how they opened at his throat and draped his broad shoulders. Liked the fact that he never took off the unusual cross that hung around his neck. Not even when he was on her therapy table.

"Why is your room half the size of the other two?"

"I don't know." He crossed his arms and sent his gaze over her. "Maybe I don't need a lot of space."

"How long have you lived here alone?"

"Five years."

"And this room, how long have you had this room?"

"Since I was born, I guess. Let's go. It's getting late."

"It's not late. It's two in the afternoon." She glanced at the bed. It had no bedspread, just a blue blanket that appeared to have been washed too many times. Leaving the box open, she crossed to the bed and sat. "My father told me the day before he died that becoming his heir makes you the richest man in Chicago. But you don't care, do you? What do you care about, Lucky?"

"You ask too many questions, Elena." He shoved away from the wall, held out his hand. "Let's go."

Instead of getting up, Elena lay down, resting her head

on one of the pillows. "Make love to me. Make love to me here." She touched the space beside her.

He dropped his hand. "Be careful, Elena."

"I don't want to be careful today."

"Get off the bed, Elena."

"I know you want to. Be my *amante,* Lucky."

He didn't answer.

"Would you be my lover if I wasn't a virgin?"

"If you think this is going to buy you another day or two at Dante Armanno, you're wrong. No more deals. No more games. I'm flying you home tomorrow night."

Elena had never thrown herself at a man before. It wasn't as easy as she'd thought it would be. She knew Lucky cared about her. Knew by the way he looked at her, by the way he wanted *on top of her,* as he'd once put it.

But suddenly she felt cheap and embarrassed. She sat up quickly, glad when her hair swung forward to hide the color flooding her cheeks. "I'm sorry," she said, then bolted past him and out the door.

"Elena!"

She wasn't going to cry, she promised herself as a ball of humiliation swelled her throat and made it hard to breathe. God, what had she been thinking, begging him like some pathetic desperate virgin?

She heard him coming after her, heard him swearing. She ran faster, determined to get away.

He caught her before she reached the stairs. Grabbing her arm, he spun her around even as he propelled her backward and up against the wall. His jaw was set and his nostrils were flared. She closed her eyes, not wanting to see his face. But it didn't matter. He was there, and she felt his warm breath as he swore at her, damning her. Damning the situation. Her father. His father. Then he was no longer saying anything as his mouth covered hers.

His hot demanding lips jolted Elena's senses. She opened her eyes, jerked her head back. "No," she protested. "No!"

"Dammit, don't say no," he demanded. "It's too late for that now."

Suddenly his hands were on her hips and he was pulling her away from the wall, cupping her backside to bring her against him. He was hard as steel, and the feel of his desire stopped Elena's struggle.

Quieter now, against her lips, he whispered, "Let me in." His mouth nipped at her upper lip, then brushed over her warm cheek. "Let me have your gift."

The power of his words, the heat of his hard body, made Elena's knees weak. His hands moved to the buttons on her black sweater, and she sank against the wall in surrender. In a matter of seconds, her sweater was open and his hands were shoving the sweater off her shoulders, revealing her sheer blue bra.

He leaned back and looked his fill as the cool air puckered her nipples. Then he was groaning and lowering his head.

The feel of his mouth on her breast sent another rush of heat into her veins. Elena bit back a strangled moan. Unable to stop herself, she arched her back and fed herself to him. "Yes," she moaned softly. "I've been dreaming of you there. Everywhere. Don't stop. *Piacere,* Lucky," she sighed. "Don't stop."

# *Chapter 10*

Lucky carried Elena back into the bedroom, then set her on her feet, his gaze searching her face for any sign that she'd changed her mind.

But there was no indication that she was anything but willing to continue what they'd started in the hallway. Her sweater was still out there, and she stood looking at him, wearing a sexy sheer bra that hid nothing from his eyes. The bra and her mother's ruby necklace.

All morning he'd been aware of her black pants hugging her hips and butt. Aware of her sexy scent and the way her black hair shone in the sunlight.

She had a beautiful face, and her body was just as beautiful. He knew that because he'd seen her naked on the beach at Santa Palazzo. He'd seen the swell of her breasts and the flare of her hips. The length of her legs. The black curls between her thighs.

Yes, he'd watched her when she was unaware he was

looking, but this time he wanted her to know he was looking.

The situation was complicated, and nothing had changed that. But he wasn't going to walk away this time. He couldn't. She wanted him, and he had wanted her since he'd seen her on the beach.

She must have thought he was going to change his mind, because she shook her head and said, "Don't think too much," then reached out and undid several buttons on his shirt.

When she leaned forward and kissed his chest, he closed his eyes, her velvety mouth causing desire to pool low in his gut. He felt her fingers free more buttons. Felt her sweet breath warm his skin.

"Elena…"

"I like the way you hold on to my name when you say it," she whispered. She sent her tongue over his nipples. "You say it like—" she looked up "—like I'm torturing you."

She had that right, Lucky thought. She had indeed been torturing him since the day he'd laid eyes on her.

He needed to get his gun out of his pants before the damn thing went off. He set her away from him, then unbuttoned the top button on his jeans and slid his hand inside. While she watched, he pulled the .22 from its warm resting place.

"Are you planning on shooting me?"

The question parted his lips in an open smile. "No, I just don't want to go off too soon."

Her innocent blush could melt snow, he thought. It had certainly melted his heart. And mushed his brains, he conceded. Why else hadn't he come to his senses yet?

He laid the gun on his dresser and stepped back close enough to touch her. To have her touch him.

She didn't hesitate. She spread his shirt wide and kissed his chest, ran her fingers along his ribs. He moaned, slid his hands over her backside and squeezed gently. "You don't act like a virgin, Elena. *Maledizione,* you make me hot."

With his words, she stopped torturing him and stepped back. "Meaning what? I'm lying?"

"No."

"Meaning I'm not shy like the others you've had?"

"No, I didn't mean that, either." He eyed the gold ring in her navel. "I couldn't say how other virgins act. I've never *had* one." She seemed surprised by his claim and that annoyed him. "Is that a problem for you? Looking for a pro the first time out?"

She backed up, folded her arms over her breasts. "You're right, maybe a pro is what I'm looking for, after all. Maybe—"

"Unzip your pants, Elena. We're going to do this. We're going to do everything, as you put it. You started this, and I'm going to finish it."

She glanced at the bed.

"You picked the place. It's too late to order a king-size and room service. Pro or not, I'm your ride. So take 'em off. Take 'em off slowly."

He backed up, reached behind him and closed the door, then leaned against it.

She did the same, backing up in the opposite direction until she met the wall. Still shielding her breasts with her crossed arms, she relaxed against it. "What if I've changed my mind?" she said softly.

"You haven't changed your mind."

Her pretty lips parted, and she shifted her eyes to his crotch. "You like to watch, don't you? Is that why you hang out at the Shedd? Why you followed me on the beach?''

''Pull 'em down, Elena.''

She uncovered her breasts and raised one long leg and unzipped her short black boot. Slow and easy, she pulled it off, then tossed it at him. He caught it and waited for the next one. It sailed across the room a few seconds later.

''Your turn,'' she said.

Her counterplay surprised him, but he dropped her boots and shoved away from the door to pull his shirt off his shoulders, then threw it at her.

She caught it. But instead of dropping it, she slipped it on and her lovely breasts became a mystery once again.

''What kind of game are you playing now, Elena?''

For an answer she unzipped her pants and pulled them down past her knees and stepped out of them. Straightening, she said, ''I'd toss them to you, but I don't think they'll fit. Your turn.''

His shirt hung to her knees, unbuttoning it allowed him a narrow strip of her lovely body to drool over. She wore black panties that rode a couple of inches below her navel. Her gold navel ring winked at him like a one-eyed tease.

He licked his lips, his craving for her triple what his thirst for Scotch had ever been. He pulled off his boots, then his socks. Standing in his jeans and nothing else, he said, ''Give me something.''

She shifted, slid her hands inside his shirt, turned her back and shimmied. When she came back around, she was holding her sheer blue bra. A second later she tossed it to him.

It was a flimsy thing, still warm and carrying her

scent. He brought it to his nose, inhaled deeply. "I like how you smell," he admitted, then shoved away from the wall. "Game over. I win."

"You win? How do you figure that?"

He came forward, his body growing as anxious as his fingers. "I win because I'm bigger than you. You have a problem with that?"

Her eyes traveled the length of his body. "Sometimes big is good. Yes?"

"*Sì*, sometimes. You ready for me?"

"I thought your job was to get me ready."

"An educated virgin." Lucky smiled, leaned forward and kissed her. "And what is your job?"

She looked him straight in the eye and said, "My job is to hang on tight and try not to pass out. I've read that the first time can produce a rush of blood to your head and make you dizzy. *Euphoria,* I believe, is the word they used."

Her wit kept him on his toes, and he liked that. He parted his shirt to expose that part of her that had been hidden from his eyes. The sight of her lush bare breasts caused him to groan.

He kissed his way down her neck and over her chest, then took one breast at a time into his mouth, sucking and stroking. Licking and tasting.

"Lucky…"

"Mm…"

"Do you have a condom with you?"

"Mm…"

"Is that a yes?"

"*Sì,*" he muttered as his mouth moved lower to her belly.

He bent his knees, tongued her navel, tugged gently on the gold ring. When his thumbs hooked the elastic of her black panties, he heard her suck in her breath. He hesitated, looked up at her. "You need a minute?"

"No. I'm…fine."

"Fine?" He slid his thumbs free and stood. "Too fast," he said, then pulled her into his arms. For the next several minutes he concentrated on her mouth and how good it felt to finally hold her. He kept it up until she began to squirm and rub herself against him, seeking more.

That's it, he thought. He wanted her hot and needy. Hungry. Not *fine*.

It was as he was considering just how hard a man could get without splitting in two, that he felt her hands slide between them and unzip his jeans. The anticipation of her hands touching him constricted his breathing. But that was nothing compared to the euphoria that spun his head the moment her fingers slipped inside his jeans and grazed the tip of him.

"Ahhh…"

"Am I hurting you?"

"In a good way," Lucky murmured. "In a very good way."

Stone-hard and aching, he pulled her along with him in the direction of the bed and laid her down, and as he joined her, he was conscious of the fact that the hours of therapy he'd spent on Elena's table allowed him to move with more ease.

He leaned over her, his hands parting his shirt so he could look at her beautiful breasts and flat stomach. Her eyes fluttered shut as his hand touched her. He lowered his head and kissed each breast, rubbed his face over her. Inhaled her sweet scent.

He couldn't get enough of her. He kissed her with slow hot kisses. Bent forward and trailed kisses down

her neck. Then back up over her chin. Her cheeks.
Nose. Eyes.

His hand slid down her stomach, grazed her navel. He
asked, "Why the ring?"

"I don't know."

He nipped her chin. "Sure you do."

"Okay, I do. I always thought it was sexy-looking."

"You don't need a ring in your navel, Elena, to look
sexy."

"You think I'm sexy?"

"I know so."

His hand moved to the edge of her panties. "Do you
have more rings anywhere else?"

She stared up at him. Smiled. "And if I say yes?"

He arched a brow. "You're joking, right?" When she
didn't answer, he said, "I guess there's only one way to
find out." His hand slid into her panties.

"Lucky—"

"Shhh. Let me touch you, Elena."

He kissed her lips, and she went still as his hand slid
into her black curls. Lower, between her legs.

She was so damn soft and he was so bone-hard. He
exhaled slowly, slid his hand lower, at the same time he
pushed his knee between her legs to spread them.

"Breathe, sweet Elena. I don't want you to pass out,"
he teased. "Not yet, anyway."

"I want this to be good for you." She sighed, her
hands moving up his chest. "I want—"

"Shhh. It's already good. Relax, and give me your
body. That's what you tell me in your therapy room.
Well, this is my therapy room."

She smiled. "And are you an expert on the subject of
making love, Lucky Masado?"

He avoided her question, not wanting any other memory to intrude on their time together. He kissed her, moved his fingers over her slit, waited to hear her suck in her breath. To hear her sweet sigh.

He stroked her, watched her face. It was all new for her—Lucky could see it in her eyes—and the reality of that slowed his movements without his being aware of it. And for the first time in his life, he wanted time to stand still. He wanted to savor the newness and the feel of her flesh. He wanted to prolong the building of heat.

He wanted to savor her gift to him.

Her fingers caressed his chest, moved over his ribs. He loved how she touched him. How inquisitive her fingers were. How hungry her mouth was every time his lips got close.

He deepened his kiss at the same time he moved two fingers into her heat. She was so hot and wet that he moaned.

In answer she said, "Noises are good."

"*Sì,* very good."

When his fingers met her barrier, he stopped and slowly withdrew.

"I'm sorry," she said, searching his face.

"No, don't be sorry for anything."

He didn't like the fact that she felt she had to apologize for being a virgin, but then, he had himself to blame. He'd called it her little problem days ago, and he regretted that now. Regretted ever making her feel inadequate.

He covered her mouth and kissed her long and deep, then whispered, "I like you brand-new. You're right. It's a gift. A gift I don't deserve."

Suddenly he rolled off the bed and stood.

"Lucky?"

He turned away, walked toward the dresser.

"Lucky?"

The panic in her voice had him turning around. She was no longer lying on the bed, but on her knees. His shirt was wrapped around her. Her eyes were wide, her black hair a wild mass around her shoulders. "Are you walking out on me?"

"No. It's too late for that, Elena." He slid open the top drawer of the dresser and found the box of condoms stored in the corner. Slipping one out, he turned around, the sealed square visible in his hand. "Too late for me to walk away, even though I know it would be the best thing for you."

He saw her relax. She came off the bed, slipping out of his shirt. "The best thing for me is you," she said, letting his shirt fall to the floor. Then she slowly pulled her panties down her hips and revealed herself to him.

The sight of her naked sent his heart to his throat. He studied her breasts, then let his eyes travel to the black curls between her legs.

"So is that all you're going to do is look?"

Her question brought him back to the bed in two strides. He set the condom on the night table, then dropped his jeans to the floor.

She drew back the blanket and sheet, then climbed beneath them. He followed her and pulled her close.

"Before you put the condom on," she whispered, "I want to touch you."

Her words turned his gut inside out, made his pulses throb hard and fast. He rolled to his back and waited for her finger to glide over his stomach to his rigid shaft. She touched without hesitation, and when she drew his sac into her hand and lowered her head, he thought he was going to die. Her mouth touched him. Kissed him.

He closed his eyes, tried to breathe slowly and deeply.

When her lips threatened to send him over the edge, he reached for her and rolled her beneath him. He spread her thighs and moved into position between her legs. When she undulated her hips, he gave her his weight and let her feel him along her inner thighs.

He rocked his body against her, welcomed the way her hands moved over his backside and hips. She was pulling him closer, rubbing and stroking him. Wanting him.

He braced his arms on either side of her and slid his body upward. Parting her slightly with his bone-stiff shaft, he watched her face, knew the minute she felt the tip of him enter her.

"Relax your hips and open for me. I want to feel you suck me inside. Without the condom first. Trust me."

She relaxed her knees and arched her hips. Lucky sank into her another inch, felt her stiffen even as she tried to stay relaxed. He moved farther, her body convulsing to accommodate him, stretching as he moved deeper.

The strangled gasp she made in the back of her throat told him he'd torn through her barrier. He went still, kissing her to defuse the sting as she curled her legs around him. She kissed back, bit his lower lip and lifted her hips at the same time.

"That's it," he whispered. "Move on me, Elena. Check me out. Do you like me?"

"Oh, yes, I like you," she breathed, then slid her hand over his backside and pushed him deeper. "No, I love you," she amended. "I love the feel of you inside me."

Lucky began to move. "The condom," he groaned, afraid if he didn't reach for it soon, he never would. He slid out of her, grabbed the package and ripped it open. When he slid the latex on, she watched. He rolled back, kissed her again. She made a little welcoming noise when he entered her and began to move again. Slowly at first, then faster.

When she curled her legs around him again and urged him deeper, he began thrusting. The pleasure she gave him was overwhelming—she was sucking him dry and at the same time, filling him up.

She was right, it was euphoric.

*Do you like me?*

*I like you. No, I love you.*

Her words spun through his brain as he continued to thrust into her. She surged upward, gasped, then began to undulate and milk him. He moaned, moved faster, felt his climax building.

Her sudden cries of ecstasy kept him watching her face, wanting to see her slip over the edge. Wanting to remember every sigh and movement she made.

"That's it, Elena. Noises are good," he encouraged.

When she came apart, her soft satiated cry undid him. Her release was so powerful it pitched him into his own climax so quickly that he surrendered with a guttural growl. He bucked his hips, moved more rapidly. Harder. Deeper.

The aftermath was a spiraling effect, satiated bodies in slow motion, accompanied by heavy breathing.

He welcomed her lips moving over his face and silently telling him she was all right. He knew he should move off her. His weight had to be a burden. She had to be exhausted. Still, he couldn't bring himself to leave her, not when all he wanted to do was start over again and end up in the same place.

"Lucky?"

Still buried inside her, he levered himself up on his elbows. When he focused on her face, he noted that her lips were swollen from his kisses and her eyes were glazed with spent passion. The physical evidence of their lovemaking was no surprise to him, but her smile was.

"What are you, a masochist? I think I ripped you in two."

"It's a wonderful feeling."

"Impossible."

"Euphoric. The book was right."

He didn't read too many books, but this book she was referring to intrigued him. He was determined to get himself a copy.

He slowly slid out of her and rolled onto his back.

"I'll be right back," she told him.

He reached for her, not wanting her to leave him. "Where are you going?"

"To the bathroom."

"Why?"

"You know why."

Yes, he did. He let her go. "Hurry back."

She leaned forward and kissed him, then she did something he didn't expect. She reached for a tissue on the night table, wrapped it around his still-hard shaft and slid the condom off him. "Don't move," she told him. "I'll come back with a washcloth."

In the privacy of the bathroom, Elena saw to her physical needs, splashed water on her face, then located a washcloth and towel. Her body was still pulsing with the aftermath of Lucky's invasion, but she hadn't been lying when she said she felt wonderful.

She returned to the bedroom moments later to find him stretched out on his stomach, his arms curled around a pillow. She hadn't been gone all that long for him to have fallen asleep; still, she said nothing and laid the washcloth on the towel, then placed the towel on the nightstand.

Quietly she slipped her black panties on, then climbed back into bed. Without hesitation, she ran her hand along the fibrous scar she'd gotten to know so well the past few days. She'd been able to ease his pain, and she felt good about that. Confident that with regular sessions of massage therapy, he wouldn't need surgery.

"It doesn't repulse you?" he muttered. "It's a bad scar."

The worst she'd ever seen, Elena silently conceded. "No," she rejected. "It doesn't repulse me. It's still you, and as you know, I like you very much. All of you."

He let go of a heavy sigh. "Rub it, Elena. It feels good when you touch it."

She knew how hard it was for him to ask for help. She raised herself on her knees. "Flatten out," she instructed, and when he did, she straddled his hips.

Leaning forward, she pressed her breasts to his back, then began to kiss her way down the scar. "I'm going to give you a pleasure massage," she whispered. "How does that sound?"

"It sounds like you could end up on your back again," he murmured into the pillow.

She slid her pelvis over his beautiful backside and heard him release another sigh. As she moved her body, she moved her hands, stroking him with both.

Several minutes later, his voice low, her name thick on his tongue, he said, "Elena, we really need to go."

"Not yet. Just a little while longer. Please. I love touching you."

Ten minutes later, on a tortured groan, he reached around and lifted her off him in one easy motion and pulled her beneath him. "And I love touching you." He brushed her lips with his. "My turn. My turn to touch and look. And taste."

A noise downstairs brought Lucky fully awake in an instant. He eased away from Elena, who slept soundly. His jeans back on, he grabbed the .22 off the dresser.

In the hallway he listened to pinpoint where the noise was coming from. The house was old and the rooms were closed off. He crept down the stairs and headed for the kitchen, rewarded when he heard footsteps behind the door.

He braced himself, counted to three, then shouldered the door open and aimed the .22. "Dammit." Lucky lowered the gun quickly. "What the hell are you doing here?"

Joey finished pouring a cup of coffee, then looked over his shoulder at his brother, his eyes taking in Lucky's half-zipped jeans, then his bare feet and chest. "I told myself you wouldn't be that stupid. Not my brother. Not the smartest man I know. I guess I was wrong. How long have you been sleeping with her?"

The muscle in Lucky's jaw tightened. "It's not what it looks like, Joey."

His brother gave a harsh laugh. Shook his head. "How long, little brother?"

"Today is the first time I…that we…" He stopped himself from going on. "How did you know where to look for us?"

"Process of elimination. I got some news I need to share with you. When I called the house, Palone said you weren't there. That you and Elena had a morning meeting with Vito's lawyer. He said you hadn't come back and that you weren't answering your cell phone. I called Henry Kendler and he didn't pick up. I got worried. One of the men thought they saw your car in the neighborhood. I came looking.''

Lucky had left his cell phone in the pocket of his jacket. At the moment his jacket was in the living room, where he'd left it when he'd followed Elena upstairs.

"This isn't your style, *fratello*. You don't make messes. So what's going on?"

What was going on was that he suddenly needed a drink. Lucky opened the cupboard, pulled out a bottle of Scotch and took it with him to the kitchen table. Once his brother was seated across from him, he said, "I don't need a lecture, Joey. It's not like I planned this.''

"I'm in no position to lecture you, Lucky. But I thought the plan was to send her home. At Vito's memorial, you said she was going back at the end of the week.''

Lucky stared at the bottle. Unscrewed the cap. Licked his lips. "She's still going back. Tomorrow night.''

"Tomorrow? Today you sleep with her and tomorrow you send her home. That doesn't look too good.''

"Dammit, Joey, I told you I didn't plan this.'' Lucky rubbed his jaw. "I know what this looks like, but you know I didn't bring her here just to get her clothes off and have a little going-away party.'' He leaned forward and rested his elbows on the table. "I don't want to talk about it. She's back with Grace and Frank as of tomorrow night, and that'll be the end of it.''

"I had this conversation with Jacky a month ago. Out of sight, out of mind doesn't work, Lucky. Just ask me. There wasn't a day that went by that I didn't think about Rhea after she was gone. When you love someone—''

"Who said I love Elena?''

"She's a beautiful woman.''

Lucky snorted. "I've slept with beautiful women before, Joey. I didn't love any of them."

"This is me, *fratello*. You wouldn't have slept with her if you'd had a choice."

"I had a choice," Lucky argued.

Joey shook his head. "No, I don't think you did. I know you too well. You don't want her gone. You've been stalling sending her back ever since she showed up in town."

"I may not want her gone, Joey, but she's going. Don't worry, I'm not about to do anything stupid."

Joey let go of another harsh laugh.

"Okay," Lucky agreed, "sleeping with her was reckless. Maybe even stupid."

Joey stood and removed his leather coat, leaving him in a gray sweater and jeans, then returned to the chair. "So you haven't made her any promises?"

Lucky leaned back and ran his hands through his black hair. "I took her to Caponelli's for lunch. She wanted to see where we grew up. We ended up here. We slept together. That's it."

This time it was Joey's turn to remain silent.

"Joey, I'm sending her home tomorrow. I'm flying her back myself."

Joey stood. "I'm sorry, *fratello*. Maybe there's a way to make this work out."

"No. She's better off back at Santa Palazzo. She's not one of us, Joey. I don't want her to be a part of this. I can't change who and what I am. We both can't. But I can keep her out of this, and I will. Now, what did you have to tell me? What was your news?"

"Jacky called. Vinnie's been released from jail."

"Then the waiting is over."

"Yes. He'll come for us now. Marrying Rhea, instead

of Sophia, was a direct slap in Vinnie's face. You shooting Moody at the Shedd was unfortunate. But the real pisser will be when he hears you're Vito's heir. Vinnie's not going to want just a little revenge for the humiliation he's suffered. He'll want blood.''

"Then it's a good thing Elena's going back tomorrow. There's something I never told you,'' Lucky said, deciding it was time Vito's confession was shared with his brother. "Before Vito died, he told me he killed Carlo. I have the proof in Vito's desk back at Dante Armanno. Carlo's ring and watch. I'll hand them over to Jacky so he can close the investigation.''

Joey walked to the window, looked out. "I thought he might have done it.''

"I wasn't surprised, either,'' Lucky admitted. "But I was surprised about something else he told me.'' He screwed the top back on the bottle of Scotch without tasting it. "Vito told me he put Frank's eye out before Grace was touched at the cabin. He said Frank passed out after that, and during that time it was Vinnie who went after Grace. He said Carlo gave the order, but it was Vinnie who brutalized Grace.''

Joey turned from the window. "Frank doesn't know, does he?''

"If he was unconscious, he never witnessed the act.'' Lucky decided to part with the rest. "Vito planned to kill Vinnie as soon as he got out of jail. He asked me to take care of it for him if he died before he got the chance.''

"And of course you said yes.''

"Vinnie's scum, Joey. What would you have said?''

"I'll do it,'' Joey suddenly offered. "I'll kill him.''

"No. It's my responsibility. I made the promise, not you.''

Joey came back to the table. "I'm sick of you always doing that."

"Doing what?"

"Thinking it's your responsibility to clean up everyone else's mess."

Lucky came to his feet. "That's my job, Joey."

"Because I forced it on you."

"No, you didn't."

"I was young and angry when I called you a killer, Lucky. I didn't mean it. I didn't mean for you to have to go through life feeling like this is what you were born to do."

"We've been over this before, Joey. It is what I was born to do. What Frank taught me to do. And I'm good at it."

Joey stepped forward, got in Lucky's face. "I never meant what I said. I was a kid. I—"

"You were angry. I know. But you were also right, Joey. I killed our mother. She died giving me life. I took her from you. You had a right to hate me for that. Frank did, too. I cheated you both."

"You never cheated either of us. And I never hated you. Frank didn't, either." Joey turned away in frustration, ran his hands through his short black hair. "But you believe that, and because you do, you've been sacrificing yourself for years. It's time you stopped thinking you have to make it right."

"I can never make it right, Joey."

Joey turned slowly, his eyes locking on the visible scar on his brother's neck, and Lucky knew his brother was remembering that night in the alley when they were teenagers. Joey still blamed himself for what happened—Lucky could see it in his eyes.

He would never forget Joey's screams when the *cricca*

had laid the blade on his neck and started cutting. It was almost as though Joey was being cut.

"You think you have guilt, Lucky. What about my guilt? How do you think I feel knowing everything you do is a direct reaction to our mother's death and what I accused you of as a kid? How do you think I feel knowing that you walked into that alley that night to give your life for me?"

"You would have done the same thing, Joey. It isn't because of our mother that I stepped into that alley. It wasn't about anything that night except keeping you and Jacky breathing." When Joey said nothing, Lucky continued, "This is a waste of time, Joey. Vinnie is out of jail, and I need to make plans to move on him before he moves on us."

"Did you hear yourself? You said, *I* need to make plans. Don't you mean *we?*"

"All right, Joey. We need to make plans. Tell Jacky about Carlo, but don't mention the rest. I don't want him interfering in my promise to Vito and going cop on us now. We'll make plans later tonight. Tell Jacky to bring Hank to the tunnel around ten and we'll meet him there."

"And Elena?"

"Elena will go home tomorrow, like I said." Lucky walked away so that his brother couldn't see the mix of emotions on his face. "As Vito once said, we make our own fate. I chose mine the day I agreed to become Vito's heir. Just like Vincent D'Lano chose his fate twenty-four years ago when he victimized an innocent woman while her husband was made to watch." Lucky turned around. "And for that he will die, Joey. I gave my word to Vito, and I will honor it. Vincent D'Lano will not live to see the new year."

Lucky grabbed his jacket and cell phone the minute Joey left and called Palone. He told him that he and Elena would be home within the hour. Then he called Frank and told him to expect Elena tomorrow evening. He explained that he would be flying her back to Key West himself. No, he wouldn't be staying. It would be a quick trip. In and out, and Frank should pick her up at the airport.

When he disconnected and turned around, Elena was standing at the foot of the stairs. She was fully dressed, and she looked as beautiful as ever. Beautiful, but different. Different in a way he was responsible for. He couldn't ignore how that made him feel. If he was possessive of her before, what they had shared today only served to tighten the noose around his neck.

Apparently she'd overheard his conversation with Frank. She said, "In and out. Nicely put, Lucky. A quickie, and then a quick trip home."

"Elena don't—"

"Don't, what? Don't feel used? I don't. I wanted you. You know that." She shrugged. "I'm no longer a virgin or inexperienced, and I wanted that, too. The afternoon was well spent. What about your back? It's important to keep up with your therapy. I know it's helping. You stand straighter, move with more range of motion. Your pain is less. If I go back home, then—"

"I'll call my doctor. Have him refer me to someone. You're right about the pain. It's better, and I haven't had any problems with the paralysis in a week. I'll keep up the therapy."

"It sounds as if you have it all worked out. Good. Then you won't need me."

She had no idea how untrue that was, Lucky thought.

"We'll leave late tomorrow night. It's better to go after dark."

She nodded and headed back upstairs. Suddenly she stopped and turned back. "Was someone here earlier? I thought I heard voices."

"The radio," Lucky said without hesitation. "I was listening to the weather forecast."

"There's been so much going on since I got here that I haven't seen Rhea. I would like to see her and Nicci before I leave. What about tonight? Dinner, maybe?"

"I'll arrange it."

She started up the stairs again, stopped. But this time she didn't turn around. "*Grazie* for today, Lucky. The monkfish and the...experience."

# Chapter 11

In the back seat of his black Lincoln Town Car, Vincent D'Lano tried to ignore his bastard son Moody's pathetic whining. His son's leg was in a cast and he'd been sent home from the hospital with crutches.

"I'm eating painkillers by the handful," Moody complained. "I'm going to kill Masado and his bitch."

Vincent ignored Moody. Just the sound of his noxious voice sickened him. It was too bad, he thought, that Lucky Masado hadn't aimed a little higher and killed the worthless bastard. Every time he thought about Moody's gutless milky-blue eyes, he wanted to puke. Eyes that years ago he'd thought beautiful on Mary Ellen.

What a tricky bitch she was, Vincent thought. It wasn't enough that she'd gotten herself pregnant, but then she'd gone and died a year later, saddling him with her little blond freak.

He would have drowned the kid like an unwanted

puppy if he'd been able to get his hands on the whelp at birth.

Fate, bitches and the Masados.

It was like a damn epidemic of bad luck had crawled up his ass and put down roots.

But things were going to get better now. He'd finally been let out of jail. And best of all, Vito Tandi was dead. Yes, things were looking up.

"I can't even have sex," Moody continued to whine. "I'm in too damn much pain to even pull my pants down. Lucky Masado is going to pay for this."

What Vincent would never admit to anyone was that he'd always been impressed with the mental and physical toughness of Frank's boys. Lucky Masado had more backbone and courage than any man alive, and Joey had a talent for tripling money faster than a toothless whore. A winning combination was what they were.

"How's Sophia, boss?"

Vincent studied the back of his driver's head. Tony Roelo had been with him for ten years. He was a bulky man, with a face that could curdle milk and ham-size hands incased in black leather gloves he seldom took off. But the feature that set Tony apart from everyone else was the puckered scar on the bridge of his nose that gave the impression someone had tried to bite it off.

"Sophia's anxious, Tony," Vincent grumbled. "Upset I got out today and she didn't. Damn my lawyer for that. Martin English has made this complicated when it didn't have to be that way. We're going to have to shake him up a bit, Tony. Let him know I'm disappointed."

"Whatever you say, boss."

Vincent turned to stare out the window as the car cruised though the old neighborhood toward his brownstone mansion. "Fill me in, Tony. You have news, huh?"

"Some of the news isn't so good, boss. Lucky Masado and a black-haired woman visited Vito's lawyer this morning. They were there a little over an hour and then they ate lunch at Caponelli's. The woman with Masado fits Moody's description of the bitch that was at the Shedd the night he was shot. I took a picture of her for you. I thought you'd like to see her."

Vincent accepted the picture Tony handed back to him. When he looked at it, he blinked twice, sure his eyes were playing a trick on him. "It can't be, Tony. Grace Tandi is dead."

"Yes, boss," Tony agreed. "That's what we thought."

"Thought? I saw her take her last breath. You did, too."

"I agree that's what it looked like. I paid Vito's lawyer a visit. Henry Kendler refused to answer my questions—at first. He changed his mind after I explained to him how important it was."

"Tell me," Vincent said.

"The woman with Masado is Grace Tandi's daughter. Kendler says Frank Masado managed to get Grace Tandi to a hospital before she bled to death that night at the cabin. It looks like the rumor that Grace was pregnant was true. Only, it was Vito's baby."

"He has an heir."

"Yes, but he never knew she existed. Not until recently."

"And the will?"

"That's another surprise."

"I hate surprises, Tony."

"Lucky Masado has been named Vito's legal beneficiary. He and Elena have been living with Vito for the past week.''

''The estate is mine!'' Moody protested, driving his fist into the door panel. ''The Shedd is mine!''

Vito ignored his son's tantrum. ''And Grace?'' he said to Tony. ''Where is she?''

''Dead. Kendler told me she died a few years ago. He said Frank Masado moved Grace out of state after she was released from a Wisconsin hospital and provided for her and her daughter.''

Suddenly Vincent couldn't breathe. He had to have Dante Armanno. All his plans hinged on owning Vito's estate. ''So the Masado boys have won again,'' Vincent muttered.

''For the moment, boss,'' Tony conceded.

Vincent's lip curled. ''When is Martin English coming to see me?''

''His car is here.'' Tony pulled the Lincoln to a stop behind the lawyer's blue Jaguar. He hit the switch that unlocked the doors, then climbed out and opened the back door for his boss.

''Damn this weather.'' Vincent shivered and pulled his fedora over his bushy eyebrows as he stepped from the car. ''I hate the way my balls shrivel in cold weather,'' he complained. ''I need a vacation, Tony. Someplace warm.''

After his driver had draped his black wool coat around his shoulders, and mindless of Moody's struggles to get out of the car with his crutches, Vincent started up the flagstone walkway. When he was halfway up the steps, the door swung open and he was greeted by one of his pretty maids. He didn't remember her name, but he remembered her breasts. They were the ones he'd paid to have enlarged.

She took his coat, and he barely acknowledged her as he headed for his study. Martin English was already inside, and Vincent removed his hat as Tony pulled his coat off his shoulders. "Close the door," he told his driver.

"What about me?"

Vincent turned to look at Moody standing outside the door balancing on his crutches. "You're no use to me in that condition. Go find a maid to listen to your whining." He motioned to the maid with the expensive breasts, who stood near the stairway that led to the second floor. "Whatever your name is, see to my son."

When Moody was gone, he turned his gaze on his lawyer. "I warned you, Martin. I warned you that I would kill ya if you didn't make this mess go away. Didn't I tell ya, I'd kill ya?"

"Nicci has a cold," Rhea explained. "So I didn't want to take him out. But I'll bring him to visit you in Florida, Elena. Joey has promised to fly us to Key West in a few months."

Elena nodded. It was cold outside, and the weather forecast predicted a winter storm would be moving into the Midwest in the next forty-eight hours. If she had a three-year-old son, she wouldn't have wanted to take him out in this weather, either.

Rhea and Joey had come for dinner. Lucky had arranged it as he'd said he would. It was good to see her friend. She had missed Rhea these past weeks. "Thank you for coming. I'd planned to see you the day after I arrived in town, but—"

"I know. I'm sure it was a shock to find out that Vito was your father. I was surprised when I heard it. How are you, Elena? How are you really?"

They were in the orange bedroom, Rhea seated on the edge of the big bed. Elena feigned a smile. "I'm fine. It's been an emotional week, I can't deny that. Losing my father so soon after we met…" She shrugged. "I keep telling myself at least we had a week."

"You look exhausted."

Elena studied Rhea's pretty blond hair and blue eyes. "I'll be fine eventually. You, on the other hand, look wonderful. Marriage must agree with you."

"Joey's amazing, Elena. I have a family now. A husband and son. I've even come to think of Lucky as the brother I never had. Jackson Ward, too. And Sunni is so sweet and friendly. She and Jackson are perfect for each other. You wouldn't think so to look at her—she's very elegant looking. But they're a match made in heaven."

"Like you and Joey."

Rhea smiled. "Yes."

Elena turned to look out the window. "I'm going home tomorrow."

"Yes, I know. Joey told me. Come sit by me." Rhea patted the bed and Elena crossed to it and sat. "We really will come for a visit, I promise."

Elena took Rhea's hand. "If anything should happen to me, Rhea, I want you to know that I love you like a sister. We had great times together at Santa Palazzo."

"What do you mean, if something happens to you? What's going to happen to you?"

"Nothing." Elena released Rhea's hand and stood. "I just meant, if anything *should* happen. You know we can never guess the future."

"Elena, what aren't you telling me?"

"There's nothing, Rhea."

"I sense there is. I noticed the way you avoided Lucky at supper. Are you angry with him for some reason? You shouldn't be too hard on him, Elena. He looks rough and I know he drinks too much, but—''

"Not anymore," Elena said. "At least, I know he's trying to cut back."

"Cut back on his drinking? Are you serious? When?"

"It's been gradual, I guess. Over the past week."

"That's wonderful."

Rhea was staring at her with curious eyes. Elena said nothing.

"There's something between you two, isn't there."

"No. Of course not." She feigned another smile. "I'm glad you came to see me. So tell me your news. What's causing this glow you have besides being married to the man you love?"

Rhea's smile spread. "I'm pregnant."

"You're pregnant?"

"Yes. Joey and I are going to have another baby. I haven't told him yet. I didn't want to say anything until I was sure. I got a call from my doctor this afternoon."

Elena moved to Rhea and hugged her. "I'm so happy for you. You deserve to be happy, Rhea. If anyone does, you do."

Elena kept her smile in place as she stepped back. She wasn't going to spoil Rhea's wonderful news with her own emotional dilemma.

"I'm organizing Sunni and Jackson's wedding for New Year's. I wish you could stay. But I'll take lots of pictures and send them to you. I promise."

"The tunnel was here when Vito bought the estate," Lucky explained as he drove the four-wheel trackster, which resembled a souped-up golf cart, deeper into the underground tunnel.

"It's a piece of architectural genius," Joey said.

"It must have cost a fortune to build," Jacky added.

Joey sat next to Lucky. Jackson and Hank Mallory, Chicago's chief of police, were seated behind them.

Jackson asked, "How is Elena taking Vito's death?"

"She'll do better once she's back home." Lucky could feel Joey's eyes on him, but he refused to look his brother's way. Elena *was* going to be fine once she distanced herself from Dante Armanno.

"Lucky? Did you hear?"

"What?"

"I said I like meeting here better than the Stardust. Less chance of being seen with Mallory," Joey explained.

For weeks they had been meeting in a back room at the Stardust, and like Joey, Lucky had been uneasy about being seen with the Chicago chief of police.

Hank Mallory had labeled Joey and Lucky as undercover informants a few weeks ago, but that wasn't what they were. They simply had a mutual agenda—shutting down greedy men like Carlo Talupa and Vincent D'Lano.

Lucky brought the trackster to a quick stop and climbed out. He hit an electronic switch and a narrow section of the wall opened to reveal a lit stairway.

After Joey, Jacky and Hank Mallory followed him up the stairs, Lucky pressed another button and the door behind them closed. At the same time another one opened in front of them to reveal a passageway that led into the master bedroom.

"This place is unbelievable," Mallory said as they filed into the spacious bedroom. He spun around, his eyes scanning the room with disbelieving eyes. Finally he said, "Where's the harem?"

Lucky was in no mood for jokes. The room was over-the-top, he'd attest to that. Not at all what he was used to, but it was obvious the room had been one of Vito's passions. The room was so large it had a warm-water pool complete with its own waterfall.

"You said the tunnel was here when Vito bought the place?" Jackson clarified.

"It was built in the early twenties. Vito said he stumbled on it by accident a few years after he moved in."

A low whistle came from Jackson as he strolled toward the waterfall that fed the pool with warm water. The waterfall was fourteen feet high and had been constructed out of white limestone. "No wonder you agreed to become Vito's heir."

Lucky scowled at his friend as Jackson shrugged out of his jacket.

"Like I said, where's the harem?" Hank chuckled.

Lucky gave Hank the same look he'd given Jackson, then turned to see his brother studying the waterfall with more interest than the other two. As a kid Joey had dreamed of one day becoming an architect.

Suddenly he turned and grinned at Lucky. "I always thought you needed a hobby, little brother. Maybe you could turn the pool into a trout pond and fish from your bed." He glanced at the ridiculous oversize bed with corner posts the size of tree trunks and a carved headboard fit for an emperor.

Ignoring the teasing, Lucky reached into his pocket and pulled out a plastic bag that held Carlo Talupa's gold ring and watch. "Here, Jacky. Vito asked me to give you these. He said they would help you close the case on Carlo's murder."

"He killed him?" Hank asked.

"For months Carlo was muscling Vito into handing over his estate to Moody Trafano," Lucky explained.

"Vito knew he wasn't going to live too much longer. I think he just decided that it was time to give Carlo what he deserved."

"*Gwaak!* A meat cleaver between the eyes. *Gwaak!*"

"What the hell is that?" Jackson asked, searching the fragrant foliage that ran along the opposite end of the pool where Chansu was perched.

"That's Summ's parrot," Lucky explained. "I'm told he spends a lot of time in here during the winter because it's fifteen degrees warmer than the rest of the house."

"More like twenty-five." Joey was stripping off his long leather jacket and draping it over an elegant chair covered in purple velvet.

"Wait till I tell Ma you got a bird." Jackson headed into the garden to get a closer look at the parrot.

"He's not my bird, Jacky," Lucky countered. "Anyway, you've got a dog and—" he looked at Joey "—you've got a kid."

"This headboard is inlaid brass." Hank Mallory stood next to the big bed. He was touring the room, touching everything like an inquisitive kid. "Asian rugs and satin pillows." He sat down on the purple velvet couch and hugged a yellow pillow. "Damn, this was worth the blindfolded trip through the woods."

At first Hank had protested Lucky's insistence that he wear a blindfold until he got into the tunnel. But the alliance between them was risky on both ends. Lucky had been concerned with Hank's safety, as well as his own and that of the men and women who worked for him.

"It's getting late," Lucky said. "Let's get this business over with before midnight."

Hank came to his feet. "My men tell me that the Colombians are determined to set up a new drug network in the city. How do we find out who they're working with so we can shut them down before they get started?''

Jackson said, ''The Colombians are known for not trusting anyone. That's why they're so successful. To get that kind of information, Hank, someone will have to penetrate their organization.''

''It's done.'' Lucky turned to see three pairs of questioning eyes staring him down. ''What's the matter?''

''It's done?'' Joey asked. ''When the hell have you had time to do that?''

''I don't have any hobbies, remember?''

Joey advanced on his brother. ''I thought we agreed that you would stay out of sight for a while. Your back is—''

''Better,'' Lucky said.

Jackson darted between the two brothers. ''Take it easy, Joe.'' Over his shoulder he said, ''On your own, Lucky? Did you make contact with the Colombians yourself?''

''No. That would have been stupid.'' Lucky looked at Joey. ''I've done some stupid things recently, but that's not one of them. In this situation our window of opportunity is tight. We didn't have the luxury of time.''

''What does that mean?'' Hank asked.

Lucky eyed the gray-haired police chief, then walked over to a round table just off the corner of the pool. As he sat, he motioned to the other empty chairs. When they were all gathered around the table, he said, ''I got a phone call from New York. The organization is anxious to fill Carlo's shoes.''

Joey frowned. ''Why would they call you about that?''

Lucky shrugged. ''Maybe they value my opinion on their choice.''

"And did you give them your opinion?" Jackson inquired.

"Yes. They asked me what I thought of Armand Santo's son."

Joey leaned forward, his eyes black as he glared at his brother. "His oldest son, Dominick?"

"Yes."

"Isn't he living down South somewhere?"

Lucky nodded. "Biloxi, Mississippi."

"What do you think of him?" Jackson asked.

"We could do worse." What Lucky didn't say was that he and Dominick had similar views in many areas. They would be able to work well together. The hard puncher from Biloxi did what he had to do to survive, and though, like Lucky, he wasn't always happy about what was required of him, he was a man of honor.

"I got to know him a few years ago," Lucky said. "He came to town tracking his younger sister. She'd run away from home and had ended up here on the streets. I found her for him."

"So is Santo going to be the new boss of bosses in Chicago?" Jackson asked.

"I don't know. He's definitely in the running."

"Can we work with him," Joey questioned, "or will we be looking over our shoulders?"

"We will always be looking over our shoulders, Joey. We won't live any different no matter who steps in and takes Carlo's place." Lucky leaned back in his chair and crossed his leg over his knee, something he hadn't been able to do in more than a year without pain shooting down his spine. But there was no pain tonight, thanks to Elena. "Now, about the Colombians…"

It was snowing when Elena left the house. She would have preferred to wait for better weather, but it was now or never. She was returning to Santa Palazzo tomorrow night.

An hour ago she'd slipped into the study and found the hidden panel that led to the tunnel her father had told her about.

The tunnel had taken her to the river, and from there she had picked her way through the deep snow in the woods with the flashlight. It had taken her a long half hour to reach the road. Hitchhiking was dangerous, but again, her choices had been few. She couldn't ask Rhea to help her, and she knew Summ and Benito's loyalty was to Lucky first—as it should be.

She'd flagged down a man driving a gray pickup and fabricated a story about having car trouble on a side road. He looked to be a decent guy. Not too talkative, but generous with the heater as he drove her into the city. He'd dropped her off at a gas station, and after he'd left, she'd called a cab.

Minutes ago the cab driver had dropped her off two blocks from Vincent D'Lano's brownstone, and she now stood outside the iron gate, her heart pounding in her chest as she considered how to break into the house. Her night's escapades were far from over. She was nervous and, yes, afraid. But Romano had taught her that a little bit of fear was good. It sharpened your senses and made you keep alert. And she would need to be alert when she breached the house security.

She pulled a ski mask out of the pocket of the black sweatshirt she wore and slipped it over her head. Dressed all in black and with the skill of a cat burglar, she picked the lock on the gate and slipped inside.

It took her only a few minutes to decide where she

should enter the house. Another lock picked and she slipped inside the service entrance, then into the kitchen.

It was a little after midnight and the house staff had gone to bed. Elena turned on her flashlight and exited the kitchen. Her flashlight back in her pocket, she followed a dim hallway, wondering how many rooms she would have to search before she found Vincent D'Lano. Not too many, she hoped.

He was likely in bed on the second floor, and that thought had her searching for a stairway.

Since the moment she'd overheard Lucky talking to Joey that afternoon in the kitchen of his family home, she'd known what she had to do. The man who had brutalized her mother was still alive. Lucky had lied to her.

Her emotions high, Elena crept farther down the hallway, stopping when she heard a woman's soft crying. Her heart began to pound harder as she located the door where the sound was coming from.

She stopped outside a heavy wooden door as the woman's crying turned into pleading, followed by a gruff voice demanding she get on her knees.

Elena was so immersed in the male voice behind the door, sure it had to be Vincent D'Lano, that she didn't hear or feel a presence behind her until the barrel of a gun nudged her ribs, and the flashlight she held was snatched from her hand.

It was then that she realized someone had been following her since she'd entered the house. Or perhaps even before that.

# Chapter 12

The ski mask was jerked from her head, and Elena's black hair fell into her eyes. A moment later she was pushed onto a chair, the gun in her sweatshirt pocket removed and pocketed.

In that moment she saw a half-naked young woman scramble off the floor, tugging the open bodice of her maid's uniform together. Wiping away tears, she ran from the room.

"Close the door, Tony."

The man who had found her in the hallway walked to the door and closed it. He was the same man Elena had seen earlier that day at Caponelli's. The bulldog with the scarred nose.

A huge desk loomed in front of her and at one corner stood Vincent D'Lano. Elena had never seen him before, but she knew this man had to be him.

He was a stocky man with a wide mustache that covered his entire top lip. He was shorter than she'd imagined him to be, she realized as she studied his angular face and cold dark eyes. He wore a gray suit, shiny black shoes and too much cologne.

"Good work, Tony. Let me guess." He reached out and grabbed a handful of Elena's hair and jerked her head back to stare at her face. "Yes, you certainly look like your mother. But you are Vito's secret seed. I see it in your eyes."

Elena reacted instinctively and spit in his face.

Vincent D'Lano's reaction was just as quick. He backhanded her so fast and so hard that when he let go of Elena's hair, her head snapped back and blood flowed from her nose.

As he wiped her spit from his face, he said, "Why is it, Tony, that women are so slow to learn their place? They have no respect, and then they cry when they're punished."

His white shirt was open, exposing a hairy chest and aging waistline. His shirt wasn't completely pulled free from his suit pants, but his zipper was open and his belt was loosened.

He stepped back and zipped up his pants, cinched his belt.

Elena wiped at the blood dripping over her mouth, smearing it across her cheek. Ignoring the pain and the stinging sensation, she said, "You're dead, D'Lano. You won't live to see the new year."

He laughed, continued to stare at her. Elena knew why. He thought he was seeing a ghost.

She said, "You did it. You were the one who tortured my mother. Tried to kill her. You will die for that, you sick bastard."

"Shut up!" He backhanded her again, this time the

force splitting her cheek open. "Did she come alone?" Vincent asked his driver.

"Yes, boss, she was alone. I spotted her at the gate while I was outside having a smoke."

"Then we have all night to see what she's made of. Good. In the morning we'll call Lucky Masado and see if he wants her back after we're done with her. We'll see if he's willing to make a trade to have her back in one piece." He reached for the knife that lay on the desk and ran his finger over the four-inch blade. "Your mother squirmed and squealed like a pig when I cut her. Let's see just how tough a little bitch you really are."

Tony laughed, then said, "You think she bites like her mother?"

His words sent Elena's eyes to the driver's ugly nose. The thought of her mother fighting for her life, biting and squealing in pain, was too much, and everything Romano had taught her over the years surged forward. Quickly she gripped the edges of her chair and made a hard sweeping motion with her left leg, smacking both of Vincent D'Lano's legs just above his ankles. The force was enough to make him cry out in pain. He dropped the knife as he lost his balance.

Before he hit the floor, Elena was on her feet, spinning around to face Tony. He came at her fast, and knowing she would be no match for his strength, she dropped to her knees, grabbed the fallen knife that lay next to D'Lano's leg, then rolled away. Back on her feet, she raised the knife.

Tony grinned. "Very good, Miss Tandi. I see you've been practicing for this day."

Maybe she had, Elena thought. Maybe she had always known that one day she would be facing the man responsible for her mother's nightmare.

''Get her, Tony,'' Vincent growled, staggering back to his feet. ''I don't want to lose her.''

Elena knew the odds were against her. She had sparred with Romano for several years, become skilled in self-defense, but did she have what it would take to face two men at the same time?

She didn't think so. Not men like these two who used women, then discarded them like garbage.

With no time to think about her decision, Elena hurled the knife at the man with the scarred nose. The minute the knife left her hand, she was moving. The knife sank into his shoulder, sending him backward with a roar of surprise and pain.

His roar distracted Vincent D'Lano for a second, and in that second, Elena surged past him and sprinted to the door. She jerked it open, then raced down the hallway and past Moody Trafano who was looking at her with a confused expression on his face.

When he tried to stick out his crutch to trip her, she shoved him hard as she sprinted on her way back to the kitchen.

She heard Moody scream as he went sprawling, but it wasn't as loud as Vincent's as he ordered his henchman to chase her down. She ran faster, hearing heavy steps behind her.

She reached the kitchen door just as Vincent was yelling at the bulldog to shoot her if he couldn't stop her. She pushed the door open into the kitchen just as a gunshot followed her inside.

The room was black as coal as the door swung shut and she immediately froze, then reached into her pocket for her flashlight. But it wasn't there. Tony had taken it from her.

Elena tried to clear her head enough to retrace her

steps. When she'd entered the back door a half hour ago, she'd moved to the right. Now she moved left in hopes of finding the service entrance.

She stumbled, and the corner of the counter drove into her side. Sucking in a breath, she laid her hands flat on the marble surface and started to move around it.

The door opened, a glimpse of light from the hall shining into the room for a split second before it was gone. "I'm going to make you scream like your mama, bitch. You can count on it," the bulldog said.

She was backing up, trying not to make a sound when suddenly she felt the heat of a warm body behind her and a hand closed over her mouth.

Elena knew instantly who is was. The size and coarseness of his hand. The scent of worn leather. She closed her eyes, sagged against Lucky in relief.

He never removed his hand from her mouth, never made a sound as he backed up, taking her with him. Elena had no idea how he could move in the darkness so silently. How he could remember where to go. What to avoid. But it didn't matter. The only thing that mattered was that he was there and would get them both out of there alive.

And then…when he got her back to Dante Armanno, he was going to kill her for slipping out of the house behind his back.

Lucky had never been so angry in his life. Angry or afraid. The idea of Elena taking on Vinnie D'Lano and Tony Roelo on her own wasn't only stupid, it was suicide.

He gripped her hand and pulled her along with him as he fled out the back entrance of D'Lano's house. It was snowing with more fervor now, the first signs of the predicted winter storm that was promising a record dump of snow.

He reached into his pocket for his cell phone and hit a stored number as he kept running. The knee-deep snow slowed them down, and he felt Elena fighting to keep up with him. But he refused to let go of her, continuing to drag her behind him in a grip that hadn't eased since he'd gotten his hands on her in Vinnie's kitchen. Speaking quickly into the phone, he avoided the sidewalks and the streetlights.

A black four-door SUV squealed around a corner and sped toward them as they reached the street. "That's our ride," he growled over his shoulder. "Keep moving."

His words seemed to revitalize her and she lengthened her stride, reaching the vehicle ahead of him as it slid to a quick stop. He let go of her hand and flung open the door. Once she was inside, he scrambled in after her.

As Jackson drove them away, the warm air in the SUV made Lucky aware of just how cold it was outside. On instinct, he reached for Elena and pulled her close. She was shivering, her teeth chattering.

"There's a blanket in the back," Jackson called over his shoulder as he ran a stop sign and sailed through two more before reaching the expressway. "Either that, or you can have a real live fur coat on your lap. Mac is crazy about the ladies."

Jackson's attempt at humor fell flat. Lucky ignored the German shepherd in the front seat and went in search of the blanket.

Once he found it, he wrapped the warm wool around Elena's shoulders, his mind replaying the hour since he'd gone upstairs to check on her and found her gone.

At first he believed she was just somewhere in the house, but after an intense search, he'd sifted through the day's events in his mind. And that had led him to remember how Elena had acted in the car that afternoon when they'd driven back to Dante Armanno. She hadn't been just quiet, she'd been struggling with some inner torment. And that torment had been what she'd overheard him tell Joey in the kitchen. She'd heard him confess that it was Vincent who'd tortured Grace.

It made sense. She'd been dressed when she'd come downstairs. Dressed, with her chin high and her anger on a tight leash.

"Is she all right, Lucky?" Jackson asked.

Before Lucky could answer, Elena's chilly voice answered, "I'm fine."

"For the moment," Lucky said threateningly. "How did you get out of the house, Elena?"

"The tunnel."

"There's no way in hell."

"Not your tunnel. My tunnel."

Her words stunned him. There was another tunnel. That he had missed the second tunnel when he had taken Vito's estate apart days ago alarmed him. What else had he overlooked? "Where's the exit?"

"In the study."

He said no more. He was still having trouble breathing. A delayed reaction, he supposed—his mind and body coming together on the reality of what could have happened if he hadn't gotten to her in time.

In twenty minutes they were through the gates of Dante Armanno and pulling up in front of the house.

Jackson said, "While I was waiting to pick you up, I got a call. Henry Kendler's wife reported he never came home from the office today. What do you make of that?"

"I don't know," Lucky answered. "But I'll send someone to check it out."

"If you don't need anything else from me tonight, I'll go. If I find out something, I'll give you a call."

"Phone Joey and have him pick up the Ferrari," Lucky said. "It's parked on Cedar Avenue, a few blocks from D'Lano's house."

Jackson flipped on the SUV's inside light and turned to Elena. "Next time you decide to—" He stopped in midsentence. "Holy hell!"

The look on Jackson's face jerked Lucky's attention to Elena. The sight of her face covered in blood sent fear ripping through him. "Elena! I thought you said you were all right."

"It's just a bloody nose, Lucky."

"Let me see." He cupped her face so he could examine it, but she shoved his hand away.

"I'm fine!" In one quick move, she tossed the blanket off her shoulders and exited the SUV before he could haul her back in.

Jackson whistled. "You got your hands full with that one, bro."

"Don't I know it," Lucky said.

By the time he entered the house, Elena was striding down the hallway with Palone and Summ trailing her like guard dogs.

Lucky yelled, "My room, Elena. Now! Palone, update the men and tell them to keep their eyes open. Vincent D'Lano knows she's Vito's daughter now. Tell the men there's a chance we could get company. Not tonight, but soon." To Summ he said, "Hot tea in twenty minutes. Something other than Matcha. *Capiche?*"

He strode past them, and as Elena started to climb the stairs, he hooked her arm and ushered her to the door of his bedroom. He didn't let go of her until they were behind closed doors and Elena was halfway down the curving stairway.

When they reached the bottom, he said, "The bathroom is this way."

Again he directed her by taking her by the arm. He was so damn angry with her and yet so relieved that she was alive that he didn't know whether to hug her or shake her.

"You're hurting me."

Lucky looked down and saw how tightly his fingers were wrapped around her arm. He immediately let go and hit the switch on the wall, flooding the bathroom with bright light.

The bathroom was as grand as the bedroom. Three times the size it needed to be, with a black marble sink and gold fixtures. The shower was large enough to accommodate a family of ten.

Lucky strode quickly to the sink. "Come here, Elena."

He filled the deep sink with warm water, anxious to assess the extent of her injuries. If it was just a bloody nose, he could live with that. But if it was more…

The thought of a scar on Elena's flawless face made his gut churn, and he felt physically sick.

"I'm capable of washing my own face," she told him. "We all bleed, Lucky. You of all people should know that."

"We bleed when we're hurt, Elena. How were you hurt?" He tried to keep his voice even as he retrieved a washcloth and submerged it in the water. When he turned, she was standing in the middle of the room looking around at all the extravagance. There was even a bathtub on a granite pedestal.

She looked small and vulnerable as she stood there

with her arms wrapped around herself. She was wearing a black sweatshirt, along with the black pants she'd worn earlier in the day. They were wet to her knees.

He squeezed out the washcloth and came toward her. When he started to wash the blood from her face, she winced and turned away.

"Dammit! Hold still. I need to see how badly you're hurt."

She ignored him and walked around him to the sink. She glanced at her face just once in the mirror, then bent over the sink, cupped warm water in her hands and began dousing her face. When the blood was gone and she'd dried her face, Lucky could see a cut on her cheek, as well as the early stages of a bruise along her jaw.

The cut was no more than half an inch long, but it was deep enough to make her scar. He swore and turned away. "Why, Elena? I was going to take care of him." He turned back and their eyes locked in the mirror.

"Why did I go to Vincent D'Lano's house by myself? Is that the question?"

"*Sì*. If you overheard that it was D'Lano who hurt your mother this afternoon, then you also heard that I planned to take him out soon."

"A week ago you told me it was Carlo Talupa who was responsible for my mother's suffering. Then you said he was dead. You lied to me, Lucky. If I can't trust you, who can I trust?"

"You lied to me, too, Elena. You said you came to Chicago for your father's name and to…understand. But that's not all you came for. You came for revenge."

"You knew?"

"Honor and respect—they come from inside, Elena. Not something you can buy. You're either born with them or you're not. You said you grew up watching your mother suffer. Your confession was laced with emotion. I knew by the look on your face and the pain in your voice that you wanted more. You wanted to avenge your mother. Yes, I knew the real reason you came to Chicago, and that's why I lied. To keep you from doing something stupid.''

She turned to face him. ''Vincent D'Lano stole my mother's life, Lucky. He stole her beauty and her dignity. He took everything from her. Everything.'' She lifted her chin. ''My mother has had multiple strokes. Any one of them could have killed her. The next one might. And there will be a next one. The doctors have assured me of that.''

''You don't have to explain why you want D'Lano dead, Elena. That's why I promised your father that I would see it was done.''

''It is my responsibility, Lucky, not yours.''

''What does it matter as long as it is done?''

She lifted her chin. ''It matters because I am the daughter of a mafioso. And because I grew up hearing Mother moan in pain night after night.''

Lucky wasn't going to argue with her. She was going home as soon as the storm broke. He walked past her and turned on the shower. ''There's a robe behind the door. Summ will bring tea in—'' he checked his watch ''—ten minutes.''

Elena stripped off her clothes the minute Lucky left and closed the bathroom door. Cold and trembling inside and out, she stepped into the shower anxious for the water spray to clear her head as much as warm her body.

While the water rained down on her and the evening's events came and went in her mind, she gave way to her emotions, slumped against the shower wall and cried.

She'd had her chance to avenge her mother and she'd failed. And now she wasn't going to get another chance. She would be flown home tomorrow and then Lucky would take over.

She had no doubt that he would kill Vincent D'Lano, that he would *fix* it for her, just as he did for everyone else.

*Why is it always your responsibility?* she'd heard Joey ask as she'd hidden in the hall and listened at the kitchen door. His voice had held a mixture of frustration and anger.

She hadn't heard all of their conversation, but she'd heard the last of it. Enough to know that Joey had an enormous amount of guilt over Lucky's role in the family as the enforcer.

*You were right. I killed our mother. She died giving me life. I took her away from you, Joey. You had a right to hate me for that. Frank, too. I cheated you both.*

Elena left the bathroom ten minutes later wrapped in the black satin robe she'd found behind the door. When she entered the bedroom, she stopped and looked around. It was the first time she'd been in this room, and now that she felt calmer, she was seeing it with a mixture of wonder and curiosity.

The lights were low, and Lucky was seated on a purple velvet couch surrounded by bright yellow pillows. His eyes were closed, but his body was still tense. It was obvious he was cooling his heels just waiting to berate her for a second time over her stupidity.

There was a tea tray on the table in front of him, but no sign of Summ. The housekeeper had delivered the tea and left. Or maybe Lucky had sent her away.

He opened his eyes and stared at the cut on her cheek. She saw his jaw tighten as he sat up slowly. ''Summ brought you tea. Orange spice. She says it's one of your favorites.''

The room was warm, and Elena swept the white towel off her head and shook out her hair. The heady scent of jasmine filled her nostrils, and she looked for the source. She soon spied the garden that lined an irregularly shaped pool built into a massive white rock structure complete with its own waterfall.

She studied the waterfall that was as unbelievable as it was beautiful. There were lights set into the rocks making the water look like diamonds as it cascaded over the rocks and into the pool. The rushing sound reminded Elena of the ocean back home. Chansu was perched among the jasmine in the colorful garden.

Her gaze then swung to the enormous bed draped in a purple velvet spread with gold trim. When she looked back at Lucky, he had slid forward to pour her tea. ''Are you still angry with me?'' she asked.

''*Si*. Very angry.''

Angry or not, she knew he wouldn't hurt her. He might yell and threaten. But he would never cause her pain.

Elena came forward and settled in one of two plush purple chairs opposite the couch and curled her feet beneath her.

After Lucky handed her the cup of tea, he settled back on the couch, stretched out his legs and rested his hands behind his head. He had changed into a pair of soft worn jeans, and the pale-colored shirt he wore had been left unbuttoned. His silver cross rested on his muscular chest.

Elena longed to reach out and touch him. To curl up in his lap and fall asleep in his arms. Yes, she was angry with him, too, but not so angry that she would ever forget how he could make her feel when he touched her.

Suddenly he sat up, "I want you to repeat the conversation you had with Vinnie. I want it as close to what was said as you can remember. Word for word if that's possible."

Elena took a sip of her tea. "It was brief. He already knew who I was. I don't know how. He called me Vito's secret seed. He asked the ugly man from Caponelli's if I'd come alone."

"That would be Tony Roelo."

"They intended to keep me there all night and…and see what I was made of, is how Vincent put it. They were going to call you in the morning and see how badly you wanted me back."

Elena saw Lucky's hands ball into fists. He sat a little straighter. "What prompted Vincent to hit you? It was Vincent, right?"

"Yes. I spit in his face."

"And how did you get away?"

"I told you that Romano taught me how to use a knife. He showed me several ways to defend myself. I knocked Vincent off balance, and when he went down, I grabbed the knife that had fallen from his hand."

"The knife? You never said anything about a knife. When did he pull that?"

"When he said he was going to see what I was made of. He told me my mother squealed like a pig when he cut her." Elena lowered her eyes, the thought making her nauseous. She stared into her teacup. "I ran out the door after I stuck the knife in Tony's shoulder. I was going for his chest." She looked up. "I threw it too high. I ran back to the kitchen, the way I'd gotten in. That's when I backed into you."

"And you intended to kill Vinnie D'Lano how?"

"The .38 I brought with me."

"You had a gun?"

"Yes. I found it in the study. It was in a hidden holster bolted to the bottom of the middle desk drawer."

"And where is the gun now?"

"Tony took it away from me, along with my flashlight."

Lucky leaned back again and studied her for another several minutes. Finally he asked, "How does your face feel?"

"Better."

"You're going to have a scar."

"Not much of a one. It's barely a scratch."

"Meaning?"

"Meaning I'm not in a great deal of pain or too tired." She held his gaze.

"You want me now?"

The words, and the way he said them… Elena told herself it was all right to sleep with him one more time. Told herself it was out of selfish need, not love, that made him so irresistible, and her desire to be wrapped in his arms so necessary. But as Lucky stood and held out his hand to her, Elena knew it was all a lie. Knew that she loved him with an ache so fierce it threatened to stop her heart from beating when she thought about leaving him.

She stood and set the teacup on the table. Slipped into his arms seconds later, tugging at his shirt until he lowered his head and covered her mouth with his.

She pressed her breasts to his chest, squirmed closer as his kiss turned hot and needy. As needy as her own. Eyes closed, her softness against his hardness, she felt his hands sweep the robe off her shoulders. She moaned, angled her head as his lips brushed her neck and moved lower. "Yes," she whispered. "Touch me, Lucky. Want me."

He lifted her into his arms and carried her to the bed. He didn't speak until he'd laid her naked body on the velvet spread. Then, lowering himself to her side, he said, "I do want you, Elena. I will always want you. But know that you are going home very soon. Sooner than you think."

"But before I go, be my lover one more time." She sighed, touched his cheek. "I love feeling you inside me. When I'm gone, I'll remember, Lucky. I promise, I'll remember."

A few hours later Lucky woke Elena with a kiss, then lifted her in his arms and carried her to the pool.

"Where are we going?" she asked groggily.

"I want to show you something," he murmured.

He rounded the pool, taking the stone steps through the garden past Chansu, sleeping on his perch. As they passed, the parrot's eyes opened and he made a low chipping sound.

"Go back to sleep," Lucky muttered.

"Go back to sleep, moron," Chansu repeated.

When Elena giggled, Lucky said, "That damn bird is a nuisance."

"He's beautiful. And you like him."

"I don't like him."

"You do so." She kissed Lucky, then ran her hand over his chest to finger the cross. "I think there's a story behind this. Does it have to do with that night in the alley?"

"What do you know about that night?"

"Summ told me the story. And my father retold it to me. Joey and Jackson are alive because of you."

"The cross was a gift from Vina a few days later. We all got one. She told us that the three crossbars symbolized the three of us. That it would remind us of our loyalty to each other and the power of it."

"But you almost died."

"Joey and Jacky would have for sure if I hadn't gone to help them. Joey took a helluva beating before I got there. He's always been tougher than he looks. And the *cricca* had broken one of Jackson's arms and several of his ribs. A rib had punctured his lung."

She kissed him. "You make me feel so safe. *Grazie.*"

He started walking again, moving into the shallowest section of the pool. He needed to give her up. And he would, he told himself. As soon as he loved her once more.

"So what is it you wanted to show me?"

"You'll see."

He walked deeper into the warm pool, the water lapping at his waist as he headed for the waterfall. She clung to him and buried her face against his neck.

"Hold your breath," he instructed. "Here we go."

She did as he told her as he walked into the waterfall. The warm water rained down on them for only a few seconds, and then Lucky was standing behind the falls facing an outcropping of white rocks.

Elena raised her head, sighed. "Oh, Lucky, it's wonderful. Our own private paradise," she whispered, her voice full of pleasure.

He walked toward a large rock, perched her on it and spread her legs. "When I saw this rock, I imagined you sitting on it just like this. And me—" he fit himself into the open notch between her thighs "—right here."

"Naked," she supplied.

"*Sì,* naked and inside you."

"And when was this? How many days ago did you imagine this?"

"Several days ago," he admitted.

"Then you wanted me that day in my bedroom when you kissed me?"

"I wanted you, Elena, long before that." He kissed her, slid her forward and pressed his thick shaft against her sex. "I want you now," he muttered. "Here."

"Yes," she whispered against his mouth. "Oh, yes."

He was rock-hard and pulsing, anxious to bury himself in her once more.

The warm water had made their bodies slick and he moved against her and into her with one smooth surge. He moaned and slid deeper. "You feel so good, Elena. Make me feel good."

She pulled him closer, wrapped her legs around his hips and urged him to the hilt. "There," she sighed. "I love you there."

Lucky began to move, pumping himself into her with deep strokes. He felt her start to come apart, her need wrenching her upward, her sighs ragged with her passion. "That's it, Elena. Move on me. *Sì*, like that. Ahhh…just like that."

He picked up speed, thrusting harder and faster. Feeding her his body again and again, he watched her face as his mind focused on the sweet promise she had made him earlier.

*I love feeling you there. When I'm gone, I'll remember, Lucky. I promise, I'll remember.*

# Chapter 13

Elena refused to cry when Lucky handed her over to Frank at the airport in Key West seven hours after he'd rescued her from Vincent D'Lano's home. He had made a good argument for why she should leave sooner than planned. Vincent would move on Lucky now that he was out of jail. Most likely within the next few days.

"How is Mother?" Elena asked when she was seated next to Frank in his black BMW heading for home.

They had lingered a moment at the airport to watch Lucky's white Cessna lift into the sky. But he was gone now. Gone, but not forgotten, Elena mused, closing her eyes to envision their lovemaking behind the waterfall.

"Did you hear me, Elena? I said, Grace is anxious to talk to you."

Elena blinked her eyes open. "You said she's better?"

"Much better. You can see for yourself."

Elena said nothing.

"Are you all right?" Frank reached out and touched her arm.

She glanced at him. He was such a handsome man, patch and all. Strong and rugged like Lucky. "A bit moody, Frank. But I'll be fine."

"Is it Vito? His death?"

It was that, and so much more. But Elena simply nodded. "I don't blame you for anything, Frank. I will be forever grateful that you saved Mother that awful night."

"I'm committed to your mother for life, Elena. But it's not out of guilt, though I feel responsible for what happened that night. I love your mother. I always have. I did what I thought was right after you were born. Only now I question—"

"Don't, Frank. You did what you thought was right. And that's why I went to Chicago. To do what I thought was right."

"Lucky said you and Vito got along well."

Elena smiled, remembering their brief time together. "He's like you. He looks intimidating, but underneath, you're both pussycats."

"Did you tell him that? I can't imagine he liked being referred to as a pussycat."

"Actually I did, and he set his jaw just like you did a second ago."

Frank chuckled.

"I love you, you know that," Elena said. "But I love him, too. I'm glad I wasn't too late."

"I'm glad, too."

"This is the way it was supposed to turn out," she stated.

Elena had thought about it so often the past week, and

she did believe that things had turned out the way God intended.

"Did Vito talk about me at all?"

"He said he was grateful to you for taking care of us. I believe he'd made his peace with you before I came. But knowing what you did, how you took care of us..." Elena paused. "I think his faith was restored in a deeper sense. When he told stories about the two of you, his eyes would light up and he'd always smile."

Frank drove through the gate and steered the BMW up the driveway. In the distance, on the veranda, Elena saw her mother sitting in her wheelchair, the early-morning sun warming her face.

After Frank turned off the engine, he said, "I've talked to her, Elena. I've told Grace some things."

Elena tucked her hair behind her ear and turned a questioning look to him. "What do you mean, you told her some things?"

"Actually, she brought it up. She said, 'Elena isn't with friends, is she.' I didn't want to lie, so I told her you were in Chicago with Lucky."

"And?"

"And she knows you're not my daughter, Elena."

"You told her?"

"Yes."

"Everything?"

"No. I didn't reveal what happened to her that night at the cabin. How she was injured. I don't feel she's strong enough to hear that. But I did tell her that before her accident, she was married to someone else. I told her about Vito Tandi. That he was dying."

"And how did she take that?"

"Better than I imagined she would. She knows you

went to see Vito and that he has since passed away. She's waiting to talk to you.''

Elena leaned forward and kissed Frank's cheek. ''Thank you, Papa. Thank you for being a man of honor.''

Wearing jeans and a pale blue tank top, Elena stepped out of the car and headed for the veranda, the breeze moving her black hair, the sun warming her cheeks.

When Grace saw her, she raised her hand and waved. Elena waved back, then hurried up the veranda steps. When she reached her mother, she stopped a foot from her, surprise widening her eyes. ''Well, look at you. A new outfit and more color in your cheeks than I've seen in weeks. And you look like you've gained weight.''

Grace beamed. ''Yes. I've regained my appetite and two pounds, Lannie. Frank says if I keep eating, he'll take me on daily boat rides. I love boat rides.''

Elena leaned forward and hugged her mother's frail body with gentle hands. ''You look wonderful, Mother.''

''Frank says the extra pounds—'' Grace turned and whispered close to Elena's ear ''—have made my breasts fuller and he likes that.''

Elena straightened and saw her mother blush. Her smile widened.

''I've missed you, Lannie.''

''And I've missed you.''

Her mother studied Elena with curious eyes. ''We need to talk, don't we?''

''Yes.''

''Come sit beside me.'' Grace clasped Elena's hand the minute she sat in the chair next to her wheelchair.

They sat facing the ocean, the warm coastal breeze on their faces. By noon Grace would be wearing a wide-brimmed hat over her yellow turban, but she would still be on the veranda watching the ocean tide rush the shoreline. She loved the ocean.

"I know you went to Chicago to meet your real father before it was too late."

"Yes, I did."

"Frank says his name is Vito Tandi. That I was married to him years ago when I lived in Chicago. I don't remember him. I don't remember anything before my accident. But on Wednesday morning I felt strange. A heaviness right here." Grace touched her heart. "Frank says that was the morning your father passed away. I'm sorry, Lannie."

Elena nodded. "Me, too."

"Was he a nice man?"

"A very nice man, Mother."

"How are Frank's boys?"

Elena took a deep breath, tried to keep the emotion out of her voice. "Joey and Rhea are very happy. Nicci keeps them busy. Rhea is pregnant."

"Oh, another baby. That's wonderful. And what about Lucky? I hope he's feeling better. Frank says he has serious back problems."

"He's feeling better." Elena refused to talk about Lucky becoming her father's heir. It would be too confusing for her mother. "He's stopped drinking."

"That's good news, too. Did you like Chicago?"

"It's cold there right now. I'm told it's beautiful in the summer."

"Will you visit next summer when Rhea's baby is born?"

"Perhaps." Elena stood and walked to the railing. There were so many things she wanted to tell her mother. So many things she wasn't sure she should share. Private feelings. Desperate emotions.

"Guess what, Lannie. Frank bought a bigger sailboat. He says he's going to stock the galley so we can sleep under the stars sometimes. And guess what else? Frank's been massaging my leg just like you do. He's very good at it. Now you can work more at the hospital if you want to. And Frank says..."

By the time Lucky landed the airplane at O'Hare, the weather forecast had been upgraded. It seemed the winter snow was moving north, but for the favor Chicago was in for subzero temperatures and blizzard-condition winds.

By seven o'clock that night the temperature had dropped to minus two degrees and the wind had begun to howl. Closed in his study, Lucky put together the final information on the Colombian drug cartel for Hank Mallory, then called him on his private line. That done, he phoned Joey and asked him to pick up Jackson and come over.

A rap on the door brought his head up from the paperwork on his desk. "Come in."

Summ entered with the tea he'd ordered—Elena's favorite, orange spice. He was a fool to torture himself with things that reminded him of her, but he couldn't help it. He glanced at the bottle of perfume on the desk, the one she'd left behind in her room. As much as the familiar scent unsettled him, it soothed him, too. Just as the tea did.

"Miss *musume*."

Lucky blinked. "What?"

"I say I miss *musume*. You miss, too?"

"Yes. But she'll be happier where she is."

Summ sniffed, and her expression seemed to question that statement. "How is back?"

"Better."

"Sit straighter. Look better. Smell better, too." She headed for the door. "I bring Matcha later to help you sleep."

An hour later Joey came through the door, his jaw tight and his shoulders covered in snow. He said, "I can't find Jackson."

The news brought Lucky to his feet. "How long has he been missing?"

"He didn't go home after work. Sunni tells me Jacky always calls if he's going to be late. She says Mac started pacing the apartment and whined at the door mid-afternoon. She's scared, Lucky. I brought her over here, along with Rhea and Niccolo. Rhea told me last night that she's pregnant. Until things are settled, I figure this is the safest place for everyone."

"Congratulations on the baby. About Jacky—did you call Vina to see if he was there?"

"I called her, but there was no answer. I hate like hell to worry her."

"You think Vinnie's got him?"

Joey shrugged. "I think it's a possibility."

"There's a chance Jacky's job has just gotten him tied up somewhere."

"If that's the case, his timing stinks. Still, I think he would have called Sunni. He's always considerate of her."

Lucky walked to the window, rubbed the back of his neck, then his unshaven jaw. "Vinnie's determined to get us."

"And what better way to draw us out? Using bait is the oldest trick in the book. And he knows Jacky would be our weakness. He wants revenge, Lucky."

"He wants blood," Lucky amended. "And right now

I don't think he cares whose it is as long as they're connected to us." Lucky faced his brother. "I learned today that he's working with the Colombians. That is, he will be if he can deliver what he promised."

"And what did he promise?"

"Dante Armanno's tunnel. For the sizable operation they want to run in Chicago they need a safe place for their cache. Some place invisible to the authorities. Some place where they can store large shipments."

Joey raised his eyebrows.

"At first the connection didn't make sense to me," Lucky admitted. "Vinnie's not powerful enough to interest the Colombians. But if he could offer them something they didn't have…" Lucky shrugged. "The tunnel is the only reason they're interested in him, I'm sure of it. That's why he got Carlo Talupa to agree to make Moody Vito's heir. It wouldn't surprise me if Carlo was in on it from the beginning."

Joey tossed his leather coat onto the couch and sat on the chair facing the desk. "It makes sense. So now what?"

"First we find Jacky. I'll make a phone call and get our guys out looking for him." After Lucky made the calls and hung up, he said, "How about some orange spice tea?"

His brother looked at him as if he'd lost his mind. Lucky ignored him and poured two cups of tea, then set one of the cups in front of Joey.

Sniffing the tea, Joey asked, "So let's discuss what we'll do if Vinnie has Jacky."

"If Vinnie has Jacky—" Lucky raised his tea to his lips "—I'm going to kill him twice."

* * *

"You didn't hit her too hard, did you?"

"I don't think so, boss."

"She breathing?"

Tony Roelo bent down and searched for a pulse on the limp body at his feet. "She's alive."

"Good. Tie her hands and throw her over your shoulder and let's go." A few minutes later Vincent led the way out of the house, Tony Roelo behind him with the unconscious woman on his broad shoulder.

They'd parked out of sight and shot a dog with a silencer gun to keep themselves from being discovered.

When they reached the car, Tony asked, "Should I put her in the trunk with the other two?"

"Yes. And make it quick."

While Tony followed orders, Vincent climbed into the car, tucking his long coat around his legs, then removed his hat. He lit a cigar and began to puff away until the back seat was thick with smoke.

While waiting for Tony to deposit the woman into the trunk, he considered the next stage of his plan. He had needed a way into Dante Armanno. A way to persuade Lucky to open the gates. An easy takeover was what he wanted. But he knew there was no such thing when you were dealing with a man like Lucky Masado. He equaled ten of his best men.

Lucky was a ruthless son of a bitch, but he had one serious flaw. He was a man of honor. And loyalty to his family came before everything else. And it was what would ultimately seal his fate.

Now all he needed, Vincent mused, was the weather to cooperate.

When the driver climbed behind the wheel, Vincent said, "Turn on the radio, Tony. See if you can get an update on the weather. My plan and that trio in the trunk aren't going to do me a damn bit of good if they start closing roads or the airports.''

"Lucky, can I talk to you?"

Lucky looked up from his desk and saw Rhea standing just inside the door. He reached out and turned the light on. He'd been sitting in the dark thinking about Elena. Thinking and remembering the way she'd touched him. How he'd touched her. How sexy her voice was, and how natural it had felt to fall in love with her.

"It's late, Rhea. Why aren't you sleeping? Joey went up to bed hours ago."

"There's been no word on Jackson?"

"Not yet."

"So we just wait...and pray?"

"The men are out searching. How's Sunni?"

"Worried. She and Jackson are supposed to be married in three weeks, Lucky. This is awful."

"Jacky's alive, Rhea. I would know if he wasn't."

"That's what Joey said." Rhea came forward wrapped in a floor-length white robe, her short blond hair framing her delicate face and drawing attention to her blue eyes. "It smells good in here."

Lucky glanced at Elena's bottle of perfume on the desk. He had foolishly misted the air with it. Hoping Rhea wouldn't notice the bottle, he said, "It sounds like congratulations are in order. Joey told me about the baby."

She touched her stomach, smiled. "Yes, another baby. A playmate for Nicci. Joey seems happy about it."

"You feeling all right?"

"Yes. A little tired, but that's to be expected. Joey said you flew Elena back home in the middle of the night."

"It was overdue. Her leaving, I mean."

She studied him a moment, then her gaze shifted to the teapot. "When did you start drinking tea?"

Lucky grinned. "Summ tells me I smell better now that I've given up Scotch."

"And who's responsible for that? Elena?"

"I don't know what you mean."

"I think you should have told Elena the truth."

"What truth?"

"The truth about how you feel about her. That you love her."

Normally Lucky didn't discuss personal business, but this was Rhea. They had become close over the past few weeks. It was hard to explain how it had happened, but they had mutual feelings about family, and it had connected them quickly. He said, "Joey told you?"

"Yes. But I'd already guessed. Last night at dinner you couldn't keep your eyes off her. And after that, in Elena's room, she was emotional when I mentioned you. She tried to cover it up, but I saw."

"Saw what?"

"I believe she cares deeply for you, too. Do you believe she's in love with you? Did she tell you she was?"

Elena had said the words to him the first time they made love. He had heard them clearly, though he'd pretended not to. Sometimes, in the heat of…euphoria, a person said things they didn't really mean. It was likely the case here, for Elena hadn't repeated the words since and had barely looked at him when he'd left her at the airport with Frank.

"Love is a complicated emotion." Rhea reached for the bottle of perfume and sniffed it, then set it back on the desk.

"At Santa Palazzo," Lucky explained, "Elena will

have a normal life. Here, she would live surrounded by bodyguards and uncertainty. She deserves better than that. You do, too. But you were stubborn.''

''I love Joey. Life without him wouldn't be worth living. We all live with uncertainty. None of us knows if we'll be here tomorrow. It's true the other option might have been more amicable for someone else, and maybe it will work for Elena. But not for me. A woman has a right to make her choice, just like a man does. Don't you agree?''

Put on the spot, Lucky scowled. ''Go to bed, Rhea. It's late and you need to rest so my new nephew or niece will be born healthy.''

She rounded the desk, leaned close and kissed his cheek. ''Oh, yes, Summ's right. You do smell better. Much better.'' She straightened, smiled down at him. ''The air in here smells good, too. Good night, Lucky.''

The phone call came the next afternoon at exactly three o'clock while Lucky and Palone were sequestered in the study blueprinting their strategy with Joey. Palone handed Lucky the phone, mouthing the words, ''It's D'Lano.''

Lucky took the phone, said, ''I've been expecting your call. What's on your mind, Vinnie?''

''I have something of yours, and you have something I want.''

''And what do you have of mine?''

''Your family.''

Lucky's jaw tightened, not liking the plural implication. ''Who do you have?''

''You'll find out when we meet. Agreed?''

''*Sì*. Where?''

''There. At Dante Armanno. I want you to open the

gate and let me in. I want you to send the guards away, all of them. And pen the dogs. And I want you and your brother out front to meet me. Unarmed.''

"How do I know you have my family? Joey is standing next to me.''

"So you want proof? A hand or a foot sent to you in a brown paper bag? It could be arranged.''

Lucky's gut knotted. "That won't be necessary. When should we expect you?''

"Within the hour. Send the guards away, Lucky. My men are watching the house. *Capiche?*''

When the phone went dead, Lucky slammed it back in the cradle.

"What is it, Lucky?" Joey was no longer in his chair. Dressed in jeans and a red sweater, he stared at his brother, waiting to hear the news.

"He wants to meet with us here.''

"Here?''

"He wants us out front in an hour. Unarmed, Joey. He wants all the guards off the grounds and the dogs penned.''

"He's coming into the lion's den?'' Palone said. "He must feel pretty damn confident.''

"Which means he believes he's got us by the balls," Joey offered. "That tells me he's got Jacky.''

"It appears that way," Lucky agreed. "But he used the word *family*. Why wouldn't he have used the word *friend?*''

Joey frowned. "I don't like that.''

Feeling suddenly sick, Lucky reached for the phone and punched in Frank's private line. The phone rang eight times before he disconnected.

"Who did you try to call?'' Joey asked.

"Frank. He's not picking up.''

"You think maybe Vinnie found out about Santa Palazzo?" He swore. "Hell, call the house. Call Elena."

Lucky dialed back, this time punching in the house number for Santa Palazzo.

"Palazzo residence."

"I would like to speak to Elena, please."

"I'm sorry, she's not here."

"Where is she? This is Lucky Masado."

"I believe she's out somewhere with Mr. Palazzo. Can I take a message? They've been gone awhile."

"No, no message." Lucky hung up. "She's with Frank somewhere."

"Well, at least we know they're together and still in Key West." Joey sighed, rubbed his jaw. "We need to get Rhea and Niccolo and Sunni out of here. I thought this was the safest place for them, but now they're sitting smack in the middle of this mess, and I can't live with that."

"It's too late to move them," Lucky argued. "Vinnie's got men watching the house, checking to make sure the guards leave. If we send Rhea and Sunni out, they'll be sitting ducks. No, we don't move anyone out, Joey. That would be a serious mistake." He walked to the bookcase and pressed a button hidden behind a row of books, and the bookcase parted to reveal a dark passageway. Both Palone and Joey stared in surprise.

"Vito was a shrewd bastard," Lucky admitted. "He let me believe there was only one tunnel under the house. Obviously by the look on your face, Palone, you believed there was only one, too. This is how Elena left the house the other night to pay Vinnie a surprise visit without anyone knowing about it. It'll be a good place for Sunni, Rhea and Niccolo to hide while Vinnie's here. If things go to hell, they have a way out alive."

Joey's visible concern for his family lifted, and he nodded his approval. "I agree the tunnel is the safest place for them."

Lucky checked his watch. "We've got an hour. Let's get moving. I want to give Vinnie the welcome he deserves. Palone, round up the men and move them out, then lock up the dogs."

"Sunni?" Lucky had gone looking for Jacky's fiancée and found her standing and staring out the window in the breakfast room. Mac, Jackson's German shepherd, sat beside her.

Wearing jeans and a red silk blouse, a glass of orange juice in her hand, Sunni was a diabetic who needed to maintain a strict diet and eating schedule. She was a beautiful woman with shiny black hair and soft gray eyes. "Have you heard something?" she asked in a strong husky voice that belied her petite size.

"D'Lano called. He's coming here. I believe he has Jacky with him, but I won't know that for certain until they get here."

"I'm afraid, Lucky."

She moved to him, and he comforted her by wrapping his arms around her. Mac growled. Lucky ignored him and said, "I can't predict what's going to happen, Sunni. But know that I'm willing to do whatever it takes to return Jacky to you safely. Trust me on that."

She looked up at him, her black hair framing her face. "I do trust you. And Joey. And I trust that whatever happens is supposed to happen. I'm still afraid, but…"

"There's an escape tunnel in the house. I want you and Rhea to take Niccolo and go there. The tunnel empties out just south of River Road. A gray Lexus will be parked a quarter mile away." Lucky handed Sunni the keys to the car. "If you have to get out of the house, take the car and go."

"How will we know if we should leave?"

"If things go to hell, you'll know it. Hear it," Lucky amended. "There's an alarm system in the house and I've reset the timer. If it goes off, then you'll know you need to leave. But don't leave before six o'clock. It'll be dark then and safer. The tunnel isn't heated, and you'll need to dress warmly. And, Sunni, if you have to leave, no one stays behind. *Capiche?*"

"Yes."

"Rhea will argue with you on that, so be ready for it. I'm sending Summ with you, too." Lucky took her hands, squeezed gently. "Jacky's a lucky guy. After the wedding, I get a dance."

His comment tugged a smile from her, which was what Lucky was after. He leaned forward and kissed her cheek. Again Mac growled, and again he was ignored.

Lucky's next objective was to find Summ and convince her to go with the women. He found her talking to Palone at the top of the stairs. "I want you to go with the other women, Summ," he said as he climbed the steps. "I'm sending them to wait in the second tunnel until this is all over." When she started to object, as he knew she would, he said, "Rhea's pregnant. She'll need you to help her with Niccolo. Put together some food and blankets. Palone, help Summ get the supplies into the tunnel. Whatever they'll need, see to it. Are the guards gone?"

"Yes, sir."

"And the dogs?"

"I saw to them personally."

"Good. Get the women settled, then take your position, Palone."

Vinnie D'Lano's Black Lincoln Town Car drove through the open gates of Dante Armanno at four o'clock. It was followed by a black van and two black Mercedes.

Lucky and Joey stood beneath the archway as the wind whistled around them.

Joey tugged up his leather collar against the bitter cold as the convoy pulled up. "You suppose that second car is the Colombians, Lucky?"

"It looks like it."

"Then you were right. He's decided to get involved in some serious drug running. I wonder if he knows that these boys play for keeps."

"The Colombians aren't the only ones who play for keeps, *fratello*." Lucky rolled his neck, ignored the snow that was collecting in his hair and on his shoulders.

Vinnie D'Lano climbed out of the Lincoln and waited while his driver draped his coat over his shoulders. Adjusting his fedora, he walked toward Lucky and Joey with five bodyguards, each carrying AR-70s. Next came two serious-faced Colombians dressed in a similar fashion, minus the hat. Tony Roelo walked a dozen steps behind him with Moody Trafano balancing on crutches.

"Where's my family?" Lucky asked when D'Lano stopped two feet from him.

"They will be brought in shortly. First I want my men to search you and your brother for weapons. Then the house for any surprises you might be planning."

"Don't you trust me, Vinnie?" Lucky's grin was as cold as the windchill factor.

The older man grinned back just as coldly. "Sure I trust you, Lucky." He looked at Joey. "It's him I don't trust. Sophia sends her love, Joey. Her love and her contempt."

Lucky and Joey were patted down by two of Vinnie's men, and when they were satisfied they carried no weapons, they entered the house. Twenty minutes later the guards ushered three maids and Finch out of the house.

"Four, sir. That's all we found."

Vincent scowled at Lucky. "Where's Joey's bitch and the brat? And that funny-talking housekeeper Vito owned? And the giant called Palone?"

Lucky said, "I sent them into town with the guards."

Vincent worried his mustache, studied Lucky as if trying to decide if he was telling the truth. But Lucky knew that if Vinnie had been watching the house, he couldn't argue with the fact that a convoy of cars had left the front gate about thirty minutes ago and ended up at Masado Towers.

"Did you check everywhere?" Vincent turned back to his guards. "Did you also check the tunnel?"

"No, boss. We couldn't find the entrance."

"It's in the master bedroom," Vincent said.

"Yes, boss, but we still couldn't find it."

"No tunnel, no deal," one of the Colombians said.

"The tunnel's there," Vincent promised.

Lucky had been right. The Colombians' alliance with Vinnie hinged on Dante Armanno's tunnel. Its size was perfect, and the mouth of the tunnel was only a few hundred yards from the river. It was a natural freeway to Lake Michigan.

The good news was that Vito had mentioned only one tunnel. Certain he knew nothing about the one accessed from the study, Lucky felt confident the women were safe. He said, "Let's go inside and get these negotiations underway, Vinnie."

Vincent's grin spread, and Lucky suspected the man was already counting the money he was going to make off the Colombians. The older man said, "After you, Lucky. Take me to the room with that big fireplace in it. It's damn cold out here."

They entered the house, Lucky leading the way down the main hallway past the stairway and the floor clock that stood outside the living-room entrance. Like so many of the other rooms in the house, the living room had shiny hardwood floors, plush oriental rugs and a chandelier that was as grand and memorable as the bed in the master bedroom.

Normally sun shone through the long narrow windows, but today the sky was angry and the only warmth came from the stone fireplace along the east wall.

Lucky heard Joey grunt in pain, and he spun around to see one of Vinnie's guards drive the butt of his gun into his brother's ribs for a second time. Joey dropped to his knees, struggling to breathe. Before Lucky could counterattack, the guard raised his gun and aimed it at Lucky's head.

Lucky held up his hands, deciding that timing was everything. This certainly wasn't how he'd pictured the scenario playing out—him getting shot between the eyes two minutes into the game. He looked past the guard, gave Joey a look that indicated his thoughts, then relaxed his stance.

Because he knew D'Lano so well, knew his greed outweighed his honor, Lucky said, "I'm prepared to work this out, Vinnie. But if you hurt my family, you will never get Dante Armanno, and I know that's what you want. You need to decide here and now if revenge on me and my brother is worth more than a profitable future with—" his gaze found the Colombians "—your new friends."

"It is a weighty decision, Lucky," Vincent admitted.

Vinnie handed Tony Roelo his hat, but kept his coat. "Tony, go get his family. Then we will start…negotiating. I'm anxious to get moved into my new home."

After Tony left, Vincent crossed to stand in front of the fire and pulled off his black leather gloves.

"You're dead, Masado. Dead!" Suddenly Moody Trafano pushed away from the wall he'd been leaning against and hobbled toward Lucky on his crutches. Six feet away, he stopped and pulled a gun from his coat pocket and aimed it at Lucky's knee. "I'm going to take you down a limb at a time, you son of a bitch. And once you're dead, I'm going to marry Elena Tandi. And after I get bored with her, I'm going to put her on the catwalk at the Shedd and sell her to whoever I want, whenever I want. How does that make you feel, Lucky?"

It made him feel as though he should have aimed a little higher that night a week ago, Lucky thought. He should have killed the bastard, instead of just blowing his knee to hell.

Before Moody got a chance to pull back the hammer

on his .38, Vincent said, "Put that away before you shoot one of us by mistake!"

Moody spun around and glared at his father. "I have a right to kill him. I'll never walk without limping."

Vincent's lip curled, and he quickly strode across the room. Facing his son, he snarled, "Dante Armanno first, fool. Now go sit down and shut up."

"You said I was going to be the one to own Dante Armanno. You said I got—"

Vincent backhanded Moody. "Shut up and go sit down!"

The force knocked Moody off balance and he landed on his backside, the gun discharging and striking Lucky in the upper arm, ripping its way through his leather jacket and adding another hole.

The force sent him to his knees, the pain stealing his breath. He struggled back to his feet, gripping his arm to stem the blood flow. "Vito's will is complicated, Vinnie. Kill me and you'll never get your hands on Dante Armanno."

There was a scuffle in the hallway. Then Tony Roelo shoved Jackson Ward ahead of him into the room. Behind them walked a frightened Lavina Ward, followed by Henry Kendler. Jackson's face was a mass of bruises, and he had a bump on his forehead the size of a golf ball. Lavina and Kendler looked unharmed.

Still, the sight of his friend wearing his own handcuffs and Lavina worrying her lip put Lucky's mood in a very dark place.

Suddenly Tony hit Jackson in the back of the head and he crumbled to the floor. Lavina cried out and rushed to her son. As she cradled his head in her lap, her gaze locked first on Joey who was on the floor a few feet away, then Lucky.

When her gaze shifted to his bloody arm, then back to his face, he could see that her fear had doubled. He shook his head slowly, winked to reassure her that all was not lost, then he glanced at Henry Kendler who stood stiff as starch, his briefcase tightly gripped in both hands.

The fact that the lawyer had made the trip with Jacky and Lavina wasn't a good sign. Obviously Vincent was determined to have Dante Armanno signed over to him tonight.

Lucky couldn't let that happen. If he did, he was a dead man. More importantly, so was his family.

## Chapter 14

Elena was anxious. The weather had put their flight behind schedule, renting a car at the airport had taken longer than it should have, and the roads were slippery.

When she saw the turnoff where she'd been picked up while hitchhiking the night before, she quickly pointed. "There. Turn up there."

"Elena," Frank said, "I think you we should talk about this plan. We don't know if Vincent is inside Dante Armanno."

"I know he's there," Elena argued. "We can't reach anyone at Joey's penthouse, and you said Hank Mallory told you Jackson's been unreachable, too. Something's terribly wrong, Frank."

"All the more reason for you to stay in the car and let me go in alone."

Elena ignored Frank's ridiculous idea. She hadn't flown back to Chicago to sit in the car. "I know that Vincent D'Lano and that ugly bulldog, Tony, are at the estate. There are no guards at the gate, and the parapet on the roof is empty. There are always four guards there, day and night.''

She had told Frank about Vincent D'Lano being the one who'd beaten Grace. They'd been discussing her mother's health, then the conversation had shifted to truth and honesty. At that moment, Elena knew Frank deserved to know the truth about the past. After that, she had poured out everything. All she had learned about Vincent D'Lano, and then all she'd experienced in the past week. Including how she felt about his son.

Before she'd finished, Frank was making plans to return to Chicago.

Elena glanced at Frank as he steered the rented SUV onto River Road. He wore a black leather coat and a stocking cap that could be pulled down and turned into a ski mask on a second's notice.

They parked not far from a silver Lexus. "Whose car do you think that is?" she asked, exiting the SUV. Like Frank, Elena wore black—a sweater and pants, and tall boots to her knees. Her dark hair was stuffed beneath a rolled-up ski mask identical to Frank's.

"I don't know. So where is this tunnel entrance you told me about?"

Elena led Frank through the knee-deep snow into the woods. The brush-and-snow-covered tunnel entrance would have been easy to miss if it hadn't been for the piece of blue cloth Elena had tied to a tree next to the opening the night she'd slipped out and gone to Vincent's house.

"Here," she said, grabbing the brush and pulling it away from the entrance. "You'll need to duck your head for the first ten feet. You'll be able to stand up straight after that."

She was about to go when Frank grabbed her arm. "I want you back in the car, Elena. Nothing can happen to you."

"And nothing will, Frank. We're wasting time. Are you leading or following?" She pulled out her flashlight.

He gave her a stern look, then pulled out his own flashlight. Crouching low, he entered the tunnel, saying, "You do exactly what I say. *Capiche?*"

Three-quarters of the way along the tunnel, they heard voices. Frank stopped and motioned for Elena to hang back. He pulled a gun from his pocket, then crept forward.

Of course Elena had no intention of being left behind. She let Frank get a good ten feet ahead if her, then resumed following him, keeping her distance and being as quiet as possible.

Frank rounded a bend and Elena lost sight of him. A moment later she heard a groan, then a thud. She clicked off her flashlight and pressed close to the wall. Adrenaline pumping, she stood in the dark for several minutes before she started inching toward the bend in the tunnel.

Please, Frank, she prayed, please be all right.

She rounded the corner at the same time she turned on her flashlight. She froze at the sight of Frank sprawled on his side, his gun and flashlight on the packed dirt floor. A woman was standing over him with a large stick.

"Oh, God!" Elena gasped.

Summ, cloaked in a dark green wool shawl, turned around. "*Musume,* is that you?"

"Yes." Elena came forward quickly dropping to her knees at Frank's side.

"I knocked him out," Summ said. "I mistake him for enemy."

Elena checked Frank's pulse and found it strong. But Summ was right, she'd knocked him out, and he didn't look as though he'd be coming around anytime soon.

"Oh, no! Frank!"

Elena looked up to see Rhea, with Nicci in her arms, hurrying toward them. "He's all right," she assured her friend. "Or he will be once he wakes up and gets rid of his headache. What are you doing down here?"

"We're waiting for a signal," Summ answered.

"A signal?"

"We think Vincent D'Lano kidnapped Jackson and that he's trading him to Lucky for Dante Armanno," Rhea explained.

A glamorous black-haired woman, cloaked in a red cape, came forward. "You must be Elena."

"And you must be Jackson's fiancée, Sunni."

She nodded. "I would rather have met under different circumstances, but…"

Elena stood, reached out and touched Sunni's arm. "Don't worry. Lucky won't let anything happen to Jackson." She glanced back at Rhea, then to Nicci. Seeing Nicci's eyes wide with uncertainty, she reached for him. "Hi, sweetheart. How's my handsome man?"

Niccolo hugged her tight. "Lannie, know what? I have a daddy."

"Yes, I know, honey." Her gaze found Rhea. "So tell me how long Vincent D'Lano has been in the house and who owns the Lexus out on the road?"

"I want to see this tunnel. We have been patient long enough."

Vincent glanced at the Colombian who'd spoken to him. He was a tall man about Lucky's size with a thick black beard and mustache. "All right. I'll show you the tunnel. Then you can see for yourself why I'm the perfect partner for your operation.''

''We'll be the judge of that,'' the shorter Colombian replied.

Lucky's gaze shifted to Vina. She should never have been brought into this, he thought. Vinnie D'Lano had made a serious mistake when he'd touched Jackson's mama, just as he had when he'd hit Elena and scarred her cheek. He stared down at Jackson where he lay unconscious on the floor. Yes, tonight there would be bloodshed, but not just his own. Vinnie had crossed the line for the last time.

Vincent motioned to a guard, then to Tony Roelo and Moody. ''You three stay here with Kendler and the others.'' He motioned to the other four guards. ''You come with me. Bring Lucky and Joey. If we're not back in thirty minutes—'' he glanced at Tony ''—kill the old woman and the cop.''

Lucky led the party up the stairs to the master bedroom. Once inside, he followed the stairway. On the way to the bathroom, he flipped a switch and the passageway leading to the tunnel opened.

''See what I told you?'' Vincent said smugly. ''I came this way with Carlo once. Wait till you see the rest of it. This place is a drug dealer's dream come true. We can filter the—''

''Shudup,'' the big Colombian said, as both men moved past Vincent and Lucky into the passageway. All business, they followed the stairway seemingly impressed, but still determined to check out the facility. Lucky and Joey followed, with Vinnie and his guards bringing up the rear.

The Colombians walked past the four-wheel trackster, glanced around, then started to follow the tunnel. Lucky watched as Vincent, puffed up like a peacock said, "The tunnel is fourteen feet wide, ten feet high and half a mile long," he called after them. "I've done my homework, boys. We can move the stash in and out nine months of the year. We'll be the number-one supplier in the Midwest."

The big Colombian looked over his shoulder at Lucky, then Vincent. "If it ends up where you said it does, we have a deal, D'Lano."

Lucky said nothing, and while two of the guards remained behind with Vincent, the other two followed the Colombians deeper into the tunnel.

Vincent lit a cigar, grinning ear to ear. "Tie Joey to that post over there." He motioned to one of his guards and the man snapped to, tying Joey to the support post with a rope around his chest and one around his thighs.

Blowing smoke, Vincent sauntered over to Joey. "You shouldn't have cheated on Sophia, you son of a bitch. You should have respected our deal. I cared for you like a son, Joey, and you repaid me by insulting me and dishonoring my daughter." He motioned to the guard, and with lightning quickness, the man threw a powerful punch into Joey's stomach.

Angry, Lucky started to advance on the guard, but before he could reach him, the guard behind him drove the butt of his gun into his bleeding arm.

Caught off guard, Lucky hesitated a second before he turned, giving the guard time to raise the gun butt again. Only, this time he drove it into Lucky's lower back.

Lucky doubled over as the pain split in two directions. The horror that his legs would give out now sent a surge of panic through him. Another swift blow sent him to the floor. Then the guard was dragging him to a second support post and wrapping a rope around his chest to

secure him where he sat dazed, blood soaking his shirt
and jacket.

Vincent sauntered forward. "I almost forgot about
your aching back. It looks like Nine-Lives Lucky has
run out of lives." Laughing, he kicked Lucky in the ribs.
"Unless you want your brother diced into tiny pieces,
my hard-nosed friend, you will sign Dante Armanno
over to me within the hour. And you'll tell me where
you've hidden Elena Tandi, too. Moody has his heart set
on marrying her, but I fancy her myself. What do you
think Vito would say if he knew I was going to keep his
lovely daughter as a trophy bride in memory of him?
How do *you* feel about it, Lucky?"

Lucky tested the rope binding him by shifting his
body against the support post. How did he feel? He felt
like hell at the moment, but he also felt relieved that
Elena was three thousand miles away at a secure location
he would take to his grave if need be.

He glanced at Joey, who was now bleeding from his
mouth and his nose as the guard slowly worked him over
a punch at a time. Lucky said, "I told you I would turn
over Dante Armanno to you, Vinnie. Now stop taking
Joey apart."

"You have no bargaining power, Lucky. I've won.
You must realize that. So where is Elena Tandi? Tell
me or I'll cut your brother's fingers off one at a time.
And then I'll start on his other appendages. *Capiche?*"

Elena left the study with the German shepherd named
Mac at her side and Summ at her back. She'd wanted to
go alone, but the housekeeper had adamantly refused to
allow it.

Quietly they moved down the hallway past the
shadow boxes. Suddenly Summ, with Chansu riding her

shoulder, reached out and tapped Elena's shoulder.
When Elena turned, the housekeeper put a finger to her
lips and motioned to the box that held two large Asian
swords.

Elena nodded, and Summ eased the door on the case
open and handed one of the three-foot swords to her.
Elena grasped the heavy sword in both hands. Summ
retrieved the second sword, then they proceeded down
the hallway toward the living room.

They had just passed the stairway, moving toward the
giant floor clock outside the living-room door, when suddenly Mac trotted to the clock and began to sniff it ag-
itatedly.

Afraid he would bark and they would be discovered,
Elena pulled the dog away from the clock, but he stub-
bornly turned back. Again she attempted to pull him
away, but the big dog was as strong as he was determined.

Suddenly the wooden face of the clock began to open,
and as Elena covered her mouth to stifle a gasp, Benito
Palone stepped out.

Elena breathed a sigh of relief when she saw him, but
Palone's reaction was the opposite. He narrowed his
eyes at her, then at Summ. Finally he shook his head
and gestured for them to turn around and return to the
study.

Elena cloned his head movement, then raised her chin
and whispered, "Where is everyone?"

He pointed to the living room. "A few are in there.
Lucky and his brother are in the tunnel with D'Lano and
the Colombians. My instructions are to neutralize the
living room—" he checked his watch "—in six
minutes."

"Neutralize?"

"You will stay here," he instructed.

"No," Elena whispered. "We'll be your backup."

At first it appeared he was going to argue with her, but finally he motioned for them to get behind him and follow.

Outside the living room, they heard voices. Elena strained to hear, and she recognized Moody Trafano's arrogant drawl, as well as the gruff tones of the bulldog. Summ tapped Elena on the shoulder, then tugged on Benito's arm. When she motioned to Chansu and flapped her hand, both Benito and Elena understood. She was suggesting they send the parrot into the room as a distraction.

Benito must have liked the idea, because he nodded and smiled at Summ.

Seconds later, as expected, Chansu's arrival in the living room was both unexpected and unwelcome. Especially when he let out a squawk and swooped down on Moody Trafano's head before nearly taking Tony Roelo's ear off with his beak. He landed on the back of a leather chair while they were still yelling.

"What the hell is that?" the guard asked.

"A damn bird," Moody answered.

"*Gwaak!* Shoot the moron. *Gwaak!*"

"He talks." Tony sounded amused. "He called you a moron."

"Maybe he was talking to you," Moody snapped.

The guard said, "Ten to one I can pick him off the back of that chair with one shot."

Worried about Chansu, Elena held up three fingers, then said, "On the count of three we rush 'em." She looked at Benito. "You take the guard, I want Tony Roelo. Summ, you take out the guy on crutches."

That said, Elena shoved Benito Palone into the room and the rush was under way.

For a big man, Benito moved swiftly, toppling the guard before he could fire his gun at Chansu. They went crashing into the table in front of the couch where Henry Kendler sat clutching his briefcase.

Summ made a wild cry as she raced past Lavina Ward and Jackson. Two swipes with her sword and she'd hacked both of Moody's crutches in half. He went down hard, screaming about his knee.

Tony Roelo was standing next to the window, and he turned before Elena reached him. Seeing her, he had the audacity to grin. He slid a hand into his pocket, pulled out a gun and aimed it at her. ''I can't kill you, because the boss is interested in you. But I can wound you. And I have no problem shooting a woman. What do you say, bitch?''

''I say shoot,'' Elena challenged, raising the sword to prove her intent.

Tony laughed, then aimed the gun at Elena's right thigh, but not before she swung the sword with both hands, then let it go. The ancient weapon made a whistling noise as it whirled twice in the air before hitting Vincent's driver in the chest. Tony grunted in pain, a red stain surfacing quickly on his broad chest. He dropped to his knees almost in slow motion, his face raw with shock.

''You were a part of my mother's nightmare twenty-four years ago, you sick monster,'' Elena spat. ''Now I'm a part of yours.''

The gun dropped from Tony's hand, and like Moody's .38, the gun's hair trigger discharged. The bullet whizzed past Elena and as Tony sank to the floor clutching his chest, she turned to see Benito hobbling toward her, gripping his thigh. His hand was covered in blood, and she realized then that the stray bullet from Tony's gun had missed her, but not Benito.

"Oh, God!" She rushed to him, aware that the room was quiet and that the guard and Moody Trafano were no longer a threat to them. Kneeling down, she examined Benito's wound, calling out, "Summ, are you all right?"

"Yes, *musume*. You?"

"Yes, but Benito's been shot."

"It's just a scratch," he said. "Don't worry about me."

"You're losing a lot of blood. Sit down." Elena pushed him onto the couch where Henry Kendler still sat frozen with fear. "Slide over, Henry," she instructed.

As the lawyer made room for Benito, he said, "That was amazing, Miss Tandi, the way you threw that sword. I don't think I've ever seen anything quite like it. Not even on TV. You were…"

Ignoring the lawyer's babbling, Elena grabbed his hand and pressed it on Benito's bleeding thigh. "Keep pressure on it, Henry. I'm sure if you keep Lucky's most valued bodyguard alive, there'll be a bonus in it for you."

While Mac licked Jackson's face, Lavina Ward tried to shake him awake. Elena said, "Summ, call Hank Mallory and tell him to come quickly. Then get everyone into the tunnel with Rhea and Sunni until he gets here."

"What about you, *musume?*"

"I'm going to find Lucky." She located Tony Roelo's gun, then headed for the door.

"No. You can't go alone," Benito said.

Elena ignored the bodyguard's protest. She had to find Lucky. She needed to see that he was all right. When she reached the stairs, she took them two at a time and entered the master bedroom. Gun in hand, she crept down the stairs, watchful for anything out of the ordinary. She passed the bathroom and found the hidden passage that led to the tunnel. Stepping inside, she pulled her ski mask over her face, then reached up and unscrewed the lightbulb overhead, darkening the stairway.

She felt her way down the stairs one step at a time, reaching the bottom without incident. On hearing voices, she strained to hear, aching to catch Lucky's deep baritone. But all she could make out was Vincent's nauseating laughter and someone's painful moaning.

Biting her lip, Elena moved soundlessly along the wall, determined not to let her imagination run away with her. Lucky was there, and if he was the one doing the moaning, it meant he was alive. And that was good.

She was about to step away from the wall and into the middle of the mayhem when someone behind her reached out and grabbed her arm. Gasping in surprise, she spun around in the dark as the gun was wrenched from her fingers.

"We have a deal, Vinnie. Send a guard up to get Kendler down here." As Lucky spoke, he glanced at his watch. Benito should be entering the living room about now. He was anxious to get that bloodthirsty guard away from Joey.

"That's not all I want, remember? Elena Tandi. Where is she, Lucky? Where is my future bride hiding?" Vincent pointed to the idle guard who'd been enjoying watching his companion work over Joey. "Go get the lawyer, Zeke. And make sure he brings his briefcase with him." To the other guard, he said, "Take a break, Charlie."

"You don't need Elena, Vinnie. Not if you have the estate," Lucky said.

"No, I don't need her. But I want her." He pulled a stiletto from his pocket and walked toward the post where Joey sagged against the rope that bound his chest and legs. Vincent jerked up his head and pointed the knife at Joey's right eye. "Once more, Lucky. Where is Elena Tandi?"

"I'm over here, Vince."

Her voice jerked Lucky's head around. Elena appeared like a mirage in the tunnel entrance. He blinked, then blinked again. For a second he wondered if the loss of blood from his gunshot wound was making him muddy-headed. He'd given Frank strict instructions not to let Elena out of his sight at Santa Palazzo for fear that she might try to return to Chicago. And now here she was!

She came forward, looking like a cat burglar on a midnight prowl. Dressed in tight black pants and a black sweater that clung to her breasts like a second skin, she carried no weapon, her hands relaxed at her sides, her beautiful hair moving around her shoulders like a storm cloud.

Vincent spun on his heel, his wool coat moving around him like a phantom's cape. Grinning, he said, "So we meet again, my lovely Elena. You are definitely your mother's daughter. I thought that from the moment I first laid eyes on you. Yes, Grace was a lovely woman. It was too bad what happened to her. But—" he shrugged "—a whore shouldn't be so choosy. That's what I told her the day I learned she and Frank were seeing each other behind Vito's back. I proposed that she and I should get to know each other a little better, too. Only, she refused me. No one refuses me, Elena. That will be the first lesson you will learn as my wife.''

Lucky saw Elena stiffen ever so slightly. She stopped ten feet from Vincent and planted a hand on her hip. ''Is that a proposal, Vince?''

''No, Elena, it's a certainty if you want to walk out of here alive.'' He motioned to Lucky. ''Either way, he's dead.''

''That's what I thought.'' She glanced at Lucky where he sat tied to the post. ''He has a point, you know. You're going to be dead in a few minutes, and he's—'' she smiled at Vincent ''—going to be rich. What would a smart woman do, Lucky?''

Vincent threw back his head and laughed. ''Not only does she look like her mother, she has Vito's head for business.''

''So it seems,'' Lucky said tightly. ''I always said that women and money have a lot in common. Here one day, gone the next.''

''Don't be a sore loser, Lucky,'' Vincent taunted.

Elena looked back at Lucky, her eyes going to the blood that continued to ooze out the hole in his leather jacket. Next, she eyed the guard lingering by Joey's beaten body. When her gaze returned to Vincent, she said, ''Death or marriage to a vengeful man with no honor… Vince, I think that's no choice at all. I would rather kill myself than let you touch me.''

Her words transformed Vincent's smile into an ugly snarl. He pointed the stiletto at her as he walked toward her. ''It's too bad you feel that way, Elena, because I will own Dante Armanno, and I will—'' he ran the knife over her breasts ''—be touching you very soon.''

''It could happen the way you say. Then again, would you ever be able to turn your back on me or close your eyes at night knowing I want you dead? That I'll be thinking about it every minute of every day?'' That said, Elena spit in his face, rewarded for her efforts with the back of Vincent's hand.

Lucky roared out his protest and fought the ropes that held him to the post.

Elena stumbled back, lost her balance and fell across Lucky's sprawled legs.

"Elena!" Lucky felt as if his heart was being ripped out of his chest.

Elena rolled onto her side to face him, blood trailing from the corner of her mouth. Slowly she dragged herself between his legs, whispered, "Jackson's waiting for a signal. He's armed with Tony's gun."

That was all Lucky needed to hear to know Vina was safe and Benito had neutralized the living room. He said, "Unzip my fly and take my gun."

"Get up, Elena," Vincent demanded. "Get up, you black-haired bitch."

"Whatever you say, Vince," Elena purred, then quickly unzipped Lucky's jeans and slid her hand inside. Her eyes met his briefly as she touched him, then slid her fingers over his flesh and between his legs. The second she felt the steel in her hand, she shoved herself to her knees, made a quarter turn and aimed the gun at the guard behind Joey. Without the slightest hesitation, she pulled the trigger and shot the guard in both legs.

The gunfire was the signal Jackson was waiting for, Lucky decided, because Jacky appeared at the bottom of the stairs like a dark angel just as the lights went out in the tunnel.

Elena dropped to the ground as a number of gunshots exploded in the tunnel. Feeling her way in the dark, she dragged herself to the post, needing to touch Lucky. He'd been shot, and the way he was sitting she suspected his legs had given out on him. She reached the post only to find him gone. For a split second she thought that maybe she'd gotten turned around and had ended up at the wrong posts. But then her hands encountered the rope that had secured him to the post.

A few minutes later the lights came back on. Blinking, Elena looked around. Lucky was nowhere in sight, and neither was Vincent D'Lano. But Jackson was at Joey's side, slicing through his rope with a knife and helping him to stand.

She rose to her feet quickly, dusting off her backside. "Where's Lucky?"

Jackson said, "I cut him loose. He must have gone after D'Lano."

"Joey, are you all right?" Elena asked.

He looked up, his face swollen and bruised. "I'll make it, Elena. What are you doing back here?"

The censure in his tone made her bristle. "I had unfinished business."

Joey braced his hands on his thighs and leaned forward, struggling to stay on his feet. "We need to find Lucky, Jacky."

A noise behind them had Elena pivoting to see Palone hobble into view. That was when she realized he must have been the one responsible for turning out the lights. He said, "We can catch him with the four-wheeler."

"Jacky and I'll run him down." Joey straightened and wiped blood from his mouth. "You take Elena to safety, Palone. Put her in the tunnel with Sunni and Rhea."

"No!" Elena shook off Palone's hand on her arm. "I want to go with you. I want—"

Joey glared at her. "You will do what I tell you. My

brother needs to know you're safe. You are a distraction, Elena. One that could get him killed. *Capiche?*''

Elena knew Joey was right. Lucky would sacrifice himself for her if need be, and she didn't want that any more than Joey did. She said, ''All right. I'll go with Benito.''

Palone tossed Joey a Beretta. ''The Colombians are still alive and so are two guards. If I turn off the lights, it might even the odds.''

''Do it,'' Joey instructed, then allowed Jackson to help him to the trackster.

# *Chapter 15*

Lucky dodged a volley of bullets from Vincent's two guards just as the lights went out for a second time. He had no idea where the Colombians or Vinnie were, but the guards had obviously been instructed to hold him off to allow their boss to get away.

He ignored the pain in his arm and moved forward as soon as the gunfire let up. Behind him he could hear the trackster's engine, then he saw the headlights. He kept close to the wall and watched as the vehicle, with Joey behind the wheel and Jackson hanging on to the back, came into view. Then he stepped out of the shadows and hopped on the back with Jackson as the four-wheeler slowed down. In a secret compartment behind the front seat, he pulled out a sawed-off shotgun and a Beretta.

Around the next corner, in the headlights of the four-wheeler, they spied the two guards running for the mouth of the tunnel. Lucky fired the *lupara* over their heads, and the two men dropped to the ground. Joey slammed on the brake, and while the trackster skidded to a stop, Jackson and Lucky jumped out and subdued the guards.

When Lucky straightened, he saw Joey holding his ribs as he climbed out from behind the wheel. Striding forward, he backed his brother up against the trackster and jerked his sweater up to see the black and purple bruises lining the right side of his rib cage. He swore, then said, "Busted ribs, Joey. You need a doctor."

Joey eyed Lucky's bloody arm. "And you don't?"

"I feel better than you look. Where's Elena? Is she all right?"

"She's fine. Palone was going to take her back to the tunnel."

Glad to hear that, Lucky said, "I'll drive."

When Joey didn't protest, he knew his brother was in a lot of pain. Making a quick decision, he climbed into the four-wheeler, turned on the ignition and before Joey or Jackson could climb in, took off.

"Lucky! Dammit, Lucky! Come back!"

Lucky never once considered turning around. He had made a promise to Vito, and for Elena's sake, he knew that she would never rest easy until the man responsible for her mother's pain had been dealt with. And then there was Joey to consider. His brother had suffered enough at the hands of Vincent D'Lano, as had his father. And Jacky and Sunni's happiness had been threatened, as well.

Lucky found the Colombians dead a few feet from the mouth of the tunnel. He hadn't expected it, and by the surprised looks on the two men's faces, neither had they.

Shot at close range, they still had their guns strapped to their shoulders.

"Play with snakes and you get bit," Lavina had always told her boys. And it was true. Vinnie was a snake, a man who would lash out at whoever got in his way.

"A *venduto*," Lucky muttered, searching for Vinnie's tracks as he stepped out into the blowing wind and knee-deep snow. The day was almost gone. In a half hour it would be dark and Vinnie would be hard to track.

Lucky picked up the trail quickly and moved into the woods at a brisk pace. He was glad for his jacket, feeling the gusty wind tear at his clothes. He shivered and tried to ignore the throbbing in his arm, knowing if Vinnie made it to the road, he'd be gone for good.

Lucky pushed himself through the snow, determined, yet suddenly uneasy. As if there was someone else in the woods besides him and Vinnie.

Fifteen minutes later he saw blood in the snow, and the sight of it made his chest tighten.

He knelt down, studying the snow around the blood. He had seen a number of knife fights, had been in many himself. He was certain that what he was looking at was the result of such a fight.

He couldn't get past the image of Elena's efficiency with a knife that night at the Shedd. Or her determination to settle the score with Vinnie on her own.

Only, Joey said Palone had taken her back to the tunnel. But there was a way into the tunnel and a way out.

The idea that Elena could be out here, that she could be the one bleeding to death at this very minute, almost buckled his legs. Heart pounding, he followed the trail of blood deeper into the woods. It was almost dark, the trees casting heavy shadows, when Lucky spied the body. He raised his *lupara* and moved toward the form dressed in black. His gut twisted and he felt his throat close off as he knelt by the body and rolled it over. Vinnie D'Lano, no longer wearing his coat, stared back at him with sightless eyes, his face cut in a familiar line that Lucky had no trouble recognizing.

Suddenly a twig snapped and he stood quickly. The *lupara* anchored against his hip, he aimed the gun, ready to shoot the first thing that moved.

Another twig snapped, and he turned in the direction of the sound. A moment later a shadow stepped out from behind a tree and started toward him.

"It was my right. My burden. Not yours, though I know you would have seen it through."

"*Sì,*" Lucky agreed. "It was your right, Frank."

Suddenly more twigs were snapping as Joey came crashing through the woods holding his ribs. Breathing hard, he jerked to a stop. He looked down at Vincent's body, then to Frank, who stood there holding a knife.

Frank said, "It was a fair fight. I gave him a knife. I gave him a chance to kill me."

Joey nodded. "Then it's over. The past is finally settled."

"Yes," Frank said. "The past is settled."

"And the future?" Joey prompted, his gaze moving to his brother.

Lucky cleared his throat. "I was going to tell you both this later, but I think now is as good a time as any. Last night I got a call from New York. They've made their decision about who they want to run Chicago."

"I take it Santo was passed over."

Lucky nodded.

Joey swore. "So who will be the new boss of bosses? Is he young or old?"

"He's not too old," Lucky offered.

"And where is he from?" Frank asked. "New York?"

"No. Right here in Chicago."

"Then we know him?" Joey asked anxiously.

"*Sì*. We know him."

"Do we like him?" Joey pressed.

"That's a hard question to answer."

"Meaning you don't," Joey grumbled, still holding his ribs. "So what's his name?"

Lucky glanced at Frank, then back to Joey. Taking a deep breath, he said, "I've been asked to fill Carlo's shoes." He waited for the words to sink in, waited for his brother to react. When neither Joey nor his father said a word, he went on, "I figure it's the best way to keep the drug cartels out of the city and work on the neighborhoods like we used to talk about, Joey. Am I wrong?"

Suddenly Frank smiled. "No, Lucky, you aren't wrong. I'd say they picked the best man for the job."

Lucky was still waiting to hear from Joey, needing his approval.

Finally his brother nodded. Then came a smile. "Papa is right. There is no better choice. You know I will support you in this. Jacky will, too. To the end and beyond, that's what we promised each other, *fratello*."

"She left with your father," Palone said.

"She's gone?" Lucky stood in his bloody shirt, staring at Benito Palone as if he was sure he'd heard wrong. They'd returned moments ago by way of the tunnel to find Jackson and Hank Mallory already in the last stages of mopping up.

Moody and Vincent D'Lano's bodyguards were already incarcerated, and Tony Roelo would be taken to the hospital first before he was put in jail.

Anxious to get back to Grace, Frank had left almost immediately. And Elena had gone with him.

Lucky still couldn't believe it. How could she have just left without saying one word to him? Was justice all she'd come back for? Well, maybe it was.

"How's your leg, Palone?"

"It's fine, sir. Sore, but I can manage."

"That'll be all," Lucky muttered. "Take the night off. You did a good job today. *Grazie.*"

"It was my pleasure to work with you, boss. What about your arm?"

"The bullet passed through it. All I need is a bandage."

Lucky paced the room after Palone left. Fifteen minutes later he stepped out into the hallway to find Summ hurrying toward him. She looked him up, then down. "Need arm fixed. Dry clothes and hot tea."

"Yes, I suppose."

"We are good team, *shujin.*"

"Yes, a good team," he replied.

"Tea in room waiting for you. I come bandage you after you take shower."

"Where's my brother and his family?"

"Upstairs in green room. Friend and fiancée in yellow room with dog. I see to their comfort. Missy Lavina in blue room."

Lucky entered the master bedroom minutes later to the scent of orange-spice tea. Unbuttoning his shirt, he descended the stairs, then entered the bathroom.

Maybe he would call Elena once she had enough time to arrive at Santa Palazzo, he mused as he stripped off his shirt and turned on the shower. Maybe he could go for a visit after Christmas. Or—

No, he knew he wouldn't do that. By leaving without saying anything, she was telling him she wanted a clean break. He had to accept that. Respect her decision.

The shower warmed him and cleaned his wound at the same time. Lucky left the bathroom minutes later with a towel wrapped around his arm, wearing a pair of black satin pajama bottoms. Ten minutes later Summ arrived to bandage his arm and deliver a second pot of tea. This one had a distinct odor: Matcha.

Once she left, he prowled the room for another hour while he considered Joey's broken ribs and the goose egg on Jacky's forehead. He didn't doubt that both men were already in a prone position and being administered to by gentle hands.

Gentle hands…

The image of Elena's hands gliding over his body stirred him. He didn't want to be tortured, but he deliberately climbed into bed, anyway, knowing that if he slept he would dream of her. Dream of her hands touching him in a dozen places.

He dozed off quickly, anxious to dream about her hands on him while she was curled up next to him.

He didn't know how long he slept. It could have been ten minutes, or an hour and ten, but when he heard the music, his first thought was that it was playing in his head and he was still dreaming. He sat up slowly, feeling the soreness in his arm, knowing it would get worse before it got better.

Begrudging the fact that he'd been woken and that Elena had been forced out of his head, he was about to lie back down, when her image appeared again—only this time he wasn't asleep.

He blinked his eyes, expecting her to disappear, but the curvy outline stayed there—there beneath the waterfall.

She was wearing a white satin slip that clung to her body.

Lucky could no longer blame the image on too much Scotch. He hadn't touched a drop in days. If Summ had spiked the tea, he was going to wring her neck.

He slid off the bed, his chest bare, the black satin pants riding low on his hips. "Elena…"

She never answered, her image suddenly disappearing behind the waterfall.

The muscle in Lucky's jaw tightened and his heart started to pound heavily inside his chest. He followed the stone path past Chansu on his perch surrounded by the fragrant jasmine. The bird's eyes opened, and he said, "Sweet dreams, moron."

Lucky ignored the bird and entered the water. Forgetting about the bandage on his arm, he headed for the waterfall and passed through it to the other side.

When he stepped out of the waterfall, Elena sighed in relief. Benito had told her that Lucky was all right, but after seeing the blood on his arm and knowing what Joey had gone through, she'd been anxious to see for herself.

Seated on the rock where they'd made love the night before, she bit her lip and waited for him to speak. She'd gone against his wishes and returned to Chicago. What would he say about that? What would he do?

He approached her, his eyes drifting to the small cut on her lip. "Where have you been, Elena?"

His voice was deep, her name so thick on his tongue that it made Elena shiver. "I rode with Frank to the airport," she said. "We talked."

He left the water, walking slowly toward the rock. "That was hours ago."

"We had a lot to discuss. How's your arm?"

"It's fine. You told Frank it was Vinnie who hurt your mother."

"Yes. I thought he deserved to know the truth."

He pulled himself up onto the rock, his pants clinging to his muscular thighs as he sat down beside her. The strength he radiated was so potent it made Elena want to melt into him.

He asked softly, "Was there another reason you told him?"

Heart pounding, Elena angled her head to look at him. He was so handsome sitting there half-naked with the silver cross nestled into the damp hair on his chest. His strong jaw was unshaven, his eyes black as midnight.

"The truth, Elena."

"All right. Yes, there was another reason. I know you promised my father that you would avenge my mother for him. But it wasn't your responsibility. I tried to do it the other night and failed." She paused, lowered her head. "I knew Frank wouldn't fail if he knew the truth."

"So you came back to finish what you'd started. But

you're still here, and the job is done. What else is there left to do, Elena? If you're wondering about your father's money, it's in a trust fund with your name on it.''

Confused, Elena frowned. ''You think I came back for money?''

He shrugged. ''As you know, I have no interest in it. I set up the trust fund at the same time I agreed to become Vito's heir. You can access the money whenever you want.''

Elena straightened her spine. ''Listen, you, I didn't come back for my father's money.''

Angry, she started to get up off the rock, but Lucky grabbed her arms, and towering over her, he forced her onto her back. ''So, Elena, why did you come back if it wasn't for Vito's money?''

''I came back to—'' she swallowed hard ''—to thank you.''

''Thank me?''

His dark eyes narrowed, and Elena felt the lump in her throat swell. She tried to clear it away. Tried again. ''You're making this difficult, Lucky.''

''On purpose, Elena. My life is difficult. It will get even more difficult in the years to come.''

''Yes, I know. Frank told me you've agreed to take Carlo Talupa's place in the *famiglia*.''

''And how do you feel about that?''

''I know you will do your best to change things. After all, you are the American Armanno. My father liked calling you that. I didn't understand why until…''

''Until?''

''Until I got to know you.''

His scowl deepened, and Elena raised her hand to

smooth it away. "*Grazie*. Thank you for showing me by example what it means to be a true mafioso, Lucky. That's what I came back to tell you."

She waited for him to say something. He wasn't going to ask her to stay, she decided. He wasn't going to say the words she longed to hear. She was in love with him. Had been from the moment she'd seen him at Santa Palazzo standing by the bar, his scarred hand clasping his famous glass of Scotch.

His gaze shifted to her breasts, where the wet satin clung to her dark nipples. "Elena," he murmured, lowering his head to brush a light kiss on her lips, "do you think that maybe you and I could—"

"Yes."

He frowned. "You say yes, even though you don't know what I was going to ask you?"

Elena took a deep breath, felt her cheeks turn hot. "Yes, I would love to feel you *there*," she admitted. "That's what you want, right? I can feel you hard against me."

He stared at her for a long moment, his frown fading. Then slowly he stood and shoved his black satin pants down his body. He returned to her, slipping between her legs, asking, "How long can you stay?"

She felt the hot tip of him move into position. "I could stay for a while. I could—"

"Share my bed?"

Oh, yes, she thought. Yes, she would love to wake up next to him. "It's a big bed," she sighed as his lips played with her mouth.

"*Sì*, it is a big bed," he agreed. "A big house." He

raised his head, looked down at her. "There would be a condition you would need to consider."

Here it comes, she thought. He was going to stipulate that when he asked her to leave, she would go without hesitation or argument. Whether it was tomorrow or next week. But what Lucky didn't understand was that she would agree to whatever he wanted as long as she could see him for an hour or a week. "I agree to the condition," she said softly.

"You do? Again, without hearing what it is?"

"Yes."

"Then should I call a priest tonight, or do you want a double wedding with Jacky and Sunni?"

"What?"

"The choice is yours."

Stunned, Elena asked stupidly, "That's the condition? You want me to marry you?"

"What did you think the condition was going to be, Elena?"

"I... You want me to live here with you as your wife?"

"That's what a wife usually does." He moved his body, slid halfway into her. "No condom, Elena. Just me, huh? Say yes. I love you, and I will keep you safe. It is my promise to you. You can trust that. You trust me, huh?"

Yes, she trusted him. Would trust him with her life. With their children's lives. She said, "Say the words again, Lucky. Say them slowly and use my name."

He sank into her fully, deeply. "I love you, Elena. I love you with my heart and my body." He bent his head and kissed her lips as the heat built between them.

"Marry me and live here at Dante Armanno with me. Live with me until…forever."

Elena ran her hands over his hips, then up his back, caressing the scar along his spine. "I love you until I ache. You are everything to me. Yes, my sexy mafioso. Yes, I will marry you and live with you forever."

"Sexy?" He grinned, then began to move his hips. "*Grazie*, Elena. *Grazie*. I promise you won't be sorry. I never go back on a promise. You know this, huh?"

"Because you are a man of honor." She sighed heavily, loving the feel of him so deep.

"*Sì*, Elena. A man of honor."

# *Epilogue*

Lucky carried the box out of the house and slid it into the back of a company van from Masado Towers. "That's the last of it," he told Joey, closing the door. "The house is empty. I have officially moved out."

Joey asked, "You're sure you want to do this?"

"I'm sure." Lucky leaned against the van next to his brother. "You said you could use another vacant house. And this one's vacant."

"Well, it won't be like we're selling it," Joey stressed. "We're just using it for the shelter. I got three boys at the moment without beds."

Lucky glanced back at the old house where they'd grown up. "There are three vacant beds upstairs. Room for more if you need it. The house could handle six or eight boys."

"Well, it just might come to that. There are new kids showing up at the shelter daily."

Joey's shelter for teenagers in need of a safe home
and a warm meal had turned into a twenty-house project,
a recreation center, with an educated staff determined to
make a difference in Little Italy—all of it funded by the
Masado brothers.

Lucky blew out a breath. It was barely dawn. New
Year's Day. Another two inches of fresh snow lay on
the ground, and the temperature was sixteen degrees.
This winter would go down in the record books as being
one of Chicago's most memorable. Snowbanks four feet
high, and windchills of minus twenty.

Yes, memorable in more ways than one, Lucky
mused, feeling better than he had in years—in body and
in spirit.

"Things are going well at the house?" Joey asked.

"Things are interesting," Lucky supplied.

"Interesting?"

"I think Palone is putting the moves on Summ."

Joey grinned. "You don't say. And Elena, how is she
doing? Keeping warm on these cold Chicago nights?"

His brother was grinning at him, and Lucky grinned
back, reminded of how he'd awoken around 4 a.m. to
Elena swimming naked in the pool, coaxing him with
that look that promised him another euphoric experience
behind the waterfall. He'd been having a lot of those
experiences lately and loving every minute. He said,
"She hasn't been complaining. How's Rhea feeling?"

"She's decorating a nursery. She's not even showing
yet, and she's buying baby quilts. I have to admit I'm
anxious, too. I missed seeing her pregnant with Niccolo." Joey shrugged. "We told him he was going to
get a playmate."

"And how did that go over?"

"He ordered a brother."

Lucky chuckled, checked his watch. "We better get going if we're going to meet Jacky for breakfast downtown. We don't want him to be late for his wedding. Sunni will skin both of us."

"Jacky wants Mac to come to the wedding. Sunni says no. She doesn't trust the dog to behave himself," Joey offered. "Father Andrew agreed. He told Jacky that the church has never had a dog in it, and it never will."

They climbed into the van, Lucky behind the wheel and Joey in the passenger seat. Lucky took one last look at the house, then started the engine. "Let's drive by Vina's house and make sure her sidewalk's been shoveled. She doesn't need one more thing to think about today. She's been in a cooking frenzy for two days."

They were only five minutes late when they pulled into the underground garage below Masado Towers. Jacky was already there waiting next to the elevator and talking to the night watchman. As they approached him, he turned and grinned. "Well, this is it. My last meal as a free man."

They entered the elevator, all three of them wearing jeans and leather jackets, their silver crosses inside their shirts.

As the elevator started to climb, Joey asked, "How's Sunni this morning?"

"She'll be fine once I stop by Silks and pick her up a few things."

Lucky raised an eyebrow, then glanced at Joey. "Sounds like Mac's been up to his old tricks again."

Jackson made a face. "He took one of Sunni's bras

to bed with him last night. It's in two pieces this morning. It's happened before, but this time it was the one she'd special-ordered to fit the neckline of her wedding dress. All I can say is it's a good thing she's started ordering three of the same thing at a time.''

"So I guess Mac won't be going to the wedding," Lucky supplied.

"No. He's going to spend a quiet day in front of the TV. I've ordered him *Westminster's Most Memorable Moments.*"

"So when's our next meeting at the house?" Jackson asked. "Hank's got a new project he wants to discuss with us. He says it's rumored another cartel wants to move in.''

Joey looked at Lucky. "Did you know about that?"

"*Sì,* I know.''

"I suppose you've already got it under control.''

Lucky's smile answered Joey's statement. "Tell Hank you'll pick him up Tuesday at nine, Jacky. But tell him not to worry about this new cartel moving in. They've changed their minds.''

"A dog in church. Did you see the look on Father Andrew's face?'' Rhea bit her lip, but her laughter escaped, anyway.

"I took pictures," Elena said.

"I want copies, okay?''

"Copies of what?'' Lucky asked as he followed Lavina into the kitchen at Caponelli's.

"Pictures of Jackson and Sunni's wedding ceremony.'' Rhea grinned. "All of it.''

"Where in heaven's name did I put the *caponata?*''

Lavina fussed. "Lucky, did you open the wine so it can breathe? And the punch, is the ice ring the bowl?"

"Wine's breathing, Vina," he assured. "And the ice is floating. Relax. From here on out, things will go smoothly."

"I wouldn't bet on it. The day has been one disaster after another."

Elena watched her husband saunter toward her wearing a black tux and a sexy smile. Yes, her husband. They had called Father Andrew the very next day after Lucky had asked her to marry him. They'd been married in a small ceremony at Dante Armanno, surrounded by Joey and Rhea and Jackson and Sunni. And of course, Lavina and Nicci, Summ and Benito, and Chansu and Mac.

Lucky slipped past Rhea and wrapped his arm around Elena. "So this is where my wife's been hiding."

She angled her head to accept his kiss. "Miss me?"

"Always."

"There will be time for that later," Lavina chastised as she located the last entrée for the buffet table. "Now come along, you three, and no more *Godfather* jokes, Lucky. Sunni's father is the chief of police in New Orleans."

"*Sì,* Vina. I know this."

"Then I don't know why you're aggravating that poor man's ulcer. He's been rubbing his stomach since he arrived in town. Oh, dear, I hope it's not my cooking."

"I'm sure it's not," Rhea soothed, taking the *caponata* from Jackson's mother. "I'll finish setting up the buffet, Lavina, while you go round up everyone for the pictures."

"Thank you, dear." Lavina smiled at Lucky and

Elena. "It was a beautiful wedding. At least it was until..." She sobered. "Do you think Sunni's parents noticed him?"

Everyone had noticed him, Elena thought. How could anyone miss a hundred-pound German shepherd belly-crawling up a thirty-foot aisle, then up four steps to crawl beneath Sunni's winter-white wedding dress, his tail sticking out one side and his nose the other.

Elena and Lucky followed Rhea and Lavina out of the kitchen. As they entered the dining room, Elena noticed Sunni on Jackson's arm, greeting their guests. They were a beautiful couple, Jackson so tall in his black tux, and slender Sunni, her black hair piled on top of her head, in white silk.

Caponelli's had occupied the same corner in Little Italy for thirty years, and the entire neighborhood had turned out for Jackson's wedding.

"Do you wish you'd had a church wedding?" Lucky asked.

Elena looked up at him. "I think our wedding was perfect." The fireplace had been blazing and she'd felt her father's presence. Yes, it had been perfect. She said, "Our wedding night was perfect, too."

"Euphoric." Lucky's hand slid over Elena's backside and pulled her close. "I sure like the way this slippery dress feels. I like the color, too. You look good in red." His gaze locked on her cleavage and the ruby that dangled between her breasts. "Wearing one of my favorite bras?" he asked softly.

Elena turned into him. "This dress," she whispered sexily, "is cut too low in both front and back to wear a bra."

He stared at her. "You mean you're not wearing one?"

Today he smelled like spicy aftershave, or maybe it was orange-spice tea. She leaned forward and ran her tongue over his lower lip, then pressed herself into him. "You tell me."

Before he could answer, Lavina called out, "I want a picture of my boys and their wives. Line up in front of the register. Come on now. Line up. Joey, get Niccolo. I want him in the picture, too."

As Joey and Lucky stood on either side of Jackson, Sunni and Rhea stepped into place in front of their husbands. Elena followed, hesitating a moment to glance up at the photo that hung behind the cash register: three small smiling boys sitting on a green couch. Years later they were still smiling, still best friends.

Beneath the photo, Elena read, *Friends to the end and beyond. Eternamente. Per sempre.*

She stepped into her rightful place in front of Lucky, and when she felt his hands glide over her hips and draw her against him, she leaned back. She felt something solid brush her backside and she angled her head to look up at her husband. "Lucky?"

"What is it, Elena?"

She arched an eyebrow at him. "That's what I'd like to know. What is it? Are you still thinking about what I'm *not* wearing, or do you have a gun in your pants?"

He smiled down at her, then gave her back her words from a moment ago. "You tell me. An experienced woman should be able to tell the difference. Especially one who knows her man as well as you do."

He nudged her gently and gave her a wolf's grin.

Elena responded by parting her lips and offering him her sexiest smile. "A man of steel," she whispered. "Every woman's dream."

"Lucky and Elena, you need to move in," Lavina insisted. "That's it. Jackson, put your arms around Joey and Lucky. Okay, now everyone smile. Good or not, this picture is going on my wall."

And it did go on Lavina's wall, *her boys* and their beautiful wives on Jackson's wedding day—along with Mac sneaking into the picture at the last minute.

*     *     *     *     *

**From *USA TODAY* bestselling author**

# EMILIE RICHARDS

### comes the story of a woman who has played life by the book, and now the rules have changed.

Faith Bronson, daughter of a prominent Virginia senator and wife of a charismatic lobbyist, finds her privileged life shattered when her marriage ends abruptly. Only just beginning to face the lie she has lived, she finds sanctuary with her two children in a run-down row house in exclusive Georgetown. This historic house harbors deep secrets of its own, secrets that force Faith to confront the deceit that has long defined her.

# PROSPECT STREET

"Richards adds to the territory staked out by such authors as Barbara Delinsky and Kristin Hannah.... Richards' writing is unpretentious and effective and her characters burst with vitality and authenticity."

—*Publishers Weekly*

*Available the first week of June 2003 wherever paperbacks are sold!*

**MIRA®**

**Coming in July 2003, only from**

# INTIMATE MOMENTS™

## Always a McBride (IM #1231)

He thought he was an only child—but he's just
found out he has four siblings. And he's inherited
their unlucky-in-love legacy—until now!

*Those Marrying McBrides!:*
**The McBride siblings have always been unlucky in love.
But it looks as if their luck is about to change....**

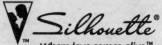

*Where love comes alive*™

**Like a spent wave,
washing broken shells back to sea,
the clues to a long-ago death had been
caught in the undertow of time...**

Coming in
July 2003

*Undertow*

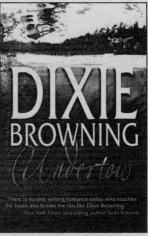

Cold cases were
Gray Hollowell's specialty,
and for a bored detective
on disability, turning over
clues from a twenty-seven-
year-old boating fatality
on exclusive Henry Island
was just the vacation he
needed. Edgar Henry had
paid him cash, given him
the keys to his cottage, told him what he knew about
his wife's death—then up and died. But it wasn't until
Edgar's vulnerable daughter, Mariah, showed up to
scatter Edgar's ashes that Gray felt the pull of her
innocent beauty—and the chill of this cold case.

**Only from Silhouette Books!**

*Silhouette*®

*Where love comes alive*™

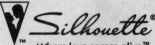